A Thirst for Vengeance

The Ashes Saga, Volume 1

By Edward M. Knight

www.edwardmknight.com

Copyright © 2014 Edwards Publishing, Ltd

ISBN: 978-0-9937370-0-8

This is a work of fiction. Names, characters, places, and incidents

Cover art by F. Bolla

First Edition: March 2014

BOOKS BY EDWARD M. KNIGHT

THE ASHES SAGA

A Thirst for Vengeance

BOOK DESCRIPTION

My name is Dagan. There are few alive with more blood on their hands than me.

I have lived a life of degeneracy. I have studied the teachings of the dark mage Helosis and walked the path of the dead. I have been to the shadowrealm and emerged with my soul enact. I have challenged the Black Brotherhood and ridden with the Knights of Valamor as a brother-in-arms. I have spoken to Xune.

I've killed indiscriminately—for money, for fame. For vengeance.

When I was young, I fell in love with a princess and was punished by her death. I have scampered, begged, and thieved. I have been homeless. I have ruled the greatest city ever built.

I began a succession war. I alone know who lifted the Seals of Regor—and how. I was there when magic was restored to this world. If I'd been born in a different age, I would have been the greatest sorcerer known to man.

My name is Dagan. This is my tale.

CHAPTER ONE

My mother was a woman as wise as she was beautiful. She was not a whore, despite stories to the contrary.

She was the eldest of five sisters born of a lord. She renounced her claim to her father's land and title when she was just sixteen. When a travelling troupe came through town, her heart was stolen by a young man with jet black hair and a singing voice that could make maidens weep.

He was my father.

My mother was a woman as wise as she was beautiful. That is why, when I was two, she tried to drive a blade of pure ivory into my heart.

But let's back up for a moment to offer some perspective on this tale.

I was born on Harvest-Bane's Eve, an ill omen if there ever was one. I was my mother's third: her third child, her third boy. As you'll soon see, the number three plays a pivotal role in my brief and miserable life.

My oldest brother, whose name need not be spoken, collapsed and died of a brain hemorrhage at age twelve. I do not know much about him, having never met him. All I know is that the blood that came from his ear made such a stain on the wood floorboards of our home that it was still there when I made my return sixteen years hence.

My middle brother, named Harry after our father, received an ill-aimed crossbow bolt through the gut when he strayed too close to a caravan fight. That was one year later. He was six. I was one.

So, perhaps it was grief that drove my mother to throw me on the table and reach for her knives. They were the only things she carried with her when she ran from home on the back of my father's horse. The hilts were gilded gold. A third of each could feed one family for three years.

But, the true value lay in the blades.

Narwhal ivory, and centuries old, inlaid with magic to prevent them from ever snapping or growing dull. The knives were a relic from an older time, when magic had not yet been forgotten.

It always astounded me that my mother would waste one on a boy such as me.

When she raised the blade over her head and uttered the words of the profane ritual that would steer her hand straight and true, a brilliant gust of wind flung the door open. Maybe it was fate that saved me that day.

But even I like to think that fate would not be so cruel.

My mother gasped, and took her eyes off me just long enough to misplace the thrust. The knife lodged into my collarbone and shattered. I carry the scar to this day.

The shock of her knife breaking reduced my mother to tears. It was confirmation of her most dreaded fear about me. My father—

"*Come on*!" the old man's voice rang out like the sound of tearing leather. "You expect us to believe your mother had *three* Narwhal ivory knives? Hoy! Who do you take us for?"

"I did not say she had three," Dagan told him calmly. He wore a hood so that only the glint of his eyes showed from beyond the shadows.

"What then? *Six*?" The old man started to laugh. He cut off with a choking sound, then swept in to show his remaining teeth in a sickening grin. "You spin a tall tale, boy. Hoy! Barkeep! More ale, eh? Keep it flowing all night, that's what I say." Without warning, the old man drew into himself. He shuddered. "Ale's the only thing keeping a man's bones warm these days."

The barkeeper was an elderly woman not unpleasant to the eye. She loaded her arms with two pitchers and carried them to the table where three men sat.

Earl, the oldest—and the drunkest—made a misguided attempt to pinch the woman's ass. It earned him a slap that sent his teeth rattling.

"So then, go on," Patch, the youngest of the group, urged. In truth, he was little more than a boy. In pleasanter times, he should have been outside chasing game or learning to ride ponies on his Da's farm. But, war has a peculiar effect that even time does not: it can turn a boy into a grown man overnight. "What did your father do?"

The hooded man tilted his head back and tasted the air. His nostrils flared the way a dog's do on the eve of a storm. "There's going to be trouble," he said, his voice flat and hollow. "You'd best get home, Patch. We'll have time enough for stories later."

Patch slouched in his seat. "It's not my fault Earl's an ass!" he sulked. "I didn't interrupt your story. Besides," his voice took on a hopeful tone, "you've been promising to tell us for weeks."

"Lad's got a point," Earl offered, reaching across the table to ruffle his hair. Patch ducked away with a scowl.

The man in the hood put both hands on the table and leaned close. "You fools aren't frightened yet, are you?" he breathed.

"Frightened?" Earl repeated. "Frightened of *what*?" He hawked up a ball of phlegm and spat it over his shoulder. "I've been on this land for nearly seventy years. I've seen war and famine. Plague and illness—the sort that come with the wind from the south. Nay, I ain't frightened of another bloody succession war. It don't concern me. Stick to your land, that's what I say. I've got no business in the realm of kings and nobility." He gave a low grunt that showed his opinion of them.

"I stay on my farm," he continued, "and ain't nobody that will bother me. The land might be a harsh mistress, but she's always given me enough to survive. Treat her well, and she won't get angry—and that's the best you can hope for from any woman, eh?" Earl chuckled and flashed his teeth at Patch. "There's some sound advice for ya. Never rouse a woman's anger. Keep that in mind, and you'll survive longer than the best sell-sword." Earl picked up his mug and took a generous swig. "Now, what do you say, Dagan?"

"I say you're a bloody fool for not being frightened." Dagan opened his eyes and turned them on Earl. The old man was no coward, but even he could not stop the unnatural chill that those eyes evoked in whoever saw them. "This is not just a succession war. When Zander moved to lift the Seals of Regor, he released things much worse than demons into this world. *Older* things."

"Like the Nehym?" Patch asked, excited. "You mean they're *real*?"

Earl reached over and clubbed Patch on the side of the head. The boy looked at him bashfully. "What was that for?"

"For believing stories your Na told you when you were suckling at her teat," Earl countered, with a lot more conviction than he felt. "Everyone knows the Nehym don't exist. Zander opened the seals half a decade ago, and I ain't seen a glimmer of difference one way or the other." He glared at the hooded man. "And you ain't either. You can go fill the boy's head with stories of riches or make-believe, but don't start pretending you know something the rest of us don't."

The hooded man's lips curled up in a rare smile. "Why, Earl," he said. "You might be a smarter man than I've given you credit for."

Earl eyed Dagan with suspicion. "Don't be mocking, now," he warned.

"I was sincere." Dagan looked at Patch. "You want a story, do you?"

"Yes, sir," Patch answered, his voice full of admiration. Remembering his manners, he added, "Please?"

"Very well," Dagan nodded. "It's not often I get a captive audience. Most people who learn my name prefer to run rather than listen." He glanced at Patch. "That should concern you."

The boy swung his head and edged closer. "Nope."

"My tale serves only one purpose," Dagan said. "And that is to teach you the folly of being a hero. My father..."

CHAPTER TWO

My father was a simple, God-fearing man. Age had robbed him of his vitality, and more recently, his hair. Patches of it still hung around his skull in long, scraggly clumps that he oiled every night. A bought of pneumonia had left his voice hoarse and cracked.

He thought it was God punishing him for absconding with my mother. I knew it was just bad luck.

My screams must have woken him that night, for there he was, standing in the gaping mouth of the farm doors like a reaper out of hell.

For all his faults, he had a practical mind. When he saw the scene before him, he threw a cloak over the table to hide me from my mother's eyes. She wept and collapsed into his arms. Together, they retreated from the room.

Like I said, my father was a simple man. He had the type of blind cunning that came up behind you and slit your throat when you were dozing off in a brothel after paying for the finest girl. It was the type of cunning that raised no qualms over stripping you bare and taking your purse after. Because, after all, dead is dead.

That is to say, he very nearly succeeded where my mother failed. When the cloak fell over my head, I could not breathe. I almost suffocated.

I do not hate him for it, for I do not think his actions came from a place of malice. They came from pervasive absent-mindedness.

Nor do I hate my mother, though I have every reason to. She was frightened. And fear can make people do desperate things.

So there I was, beneath cover on the wooden table. The cloak was cutting off my air supply, and I was squealing and paroxysizing like a gutted pig. Eventually, I exhausted myself with vain kicks and useless cries. The oxygen in my brain already low, I succumbed to a deep, coma-like sleep.

I awoke the next day in a ditch by the side of a road. My mother had had a change of heart: instead of killing me herself, she decided to let nature do it for her.

Where I lived, rabid dogs patrol the countryside. A child my size, alone and unprotected, would have made for a tasty morsel. If not the dogs, exposure would have killed me.

But I have found in myself a remarkable trait that is rare in this world. I am capable of hanging on to the edge of life for far longer than any sane man should. It is a trait that I have made use of multiple times.

I would not advise you to try.

Countless days of rolling around in the mud, crying, and being generally useless came to a blessed end when a gypsy caravan rolled by. I was picked up by an old woman closer to death than even me. Her skin was deep brown from the sun. Cracks ran along her face like fissures in the earth. The mark of gypsies in those days had been their reluctance to don clothing above their hips. Her breasts hung limp and flat all the way to her waist. Her hair had frizzled and dried ages ago. She rarely bathed.

A more foul-smelling, unpleasant woman could not be found.

Yet, I adored her as my savior. She gave me food and drink and nursed me back to health. My primitive, underdeveloped mind knew I had found a home.

My primitive, underdeveloped mind was wrong.

Two weeks later, I was handed over to a tall, thewy slaver named Three-Grin. In later years, I have heard it said that his name came from his ability to smile three times while flogging a man to death.

That was not true. His name came from the deep welts he had carved in his cheeks, giving him the impression of three grim, smiling lips.

And, for what it's worth, he smiled far more than three times when he killed his property. He enjoyed it because he thought he was giving sacrifice to the great God Xune.

However, being made a tribute was not my fate. I was left to a much crueler master:

The Arena.

Three-Grin raised children for the Arena. After being sold by the gypsy woman, I was thrown into a dungeon and forgotten.

I was not alone in that wet, dark pit. Other children made noises around me. Some gurgled. Most cried.

Even the most precocious child will cry for his mother for days on end without giving up. That sort of stark stubbornness has to be admired.

It is something I lacked entirely.

My mother had tried to kill me. The woman whom I thought replaced her handed me off to a man who dumped me underground. My life had been short, at this point, but it had also been hard.

That is to say, I knew Mother would not come. I did not cry.

That silence served me well. At first, the older children thought me dumb. Later, when they saw the spark of intellect in my eyes, they mistook it for something else:

Insanity.

One man took care of us beneath the earth. He did not speak, either. When I reflect on my time there, I now realize that he may have been mute.

He wore the same ashen gray robes every day. Perhaps he had been a child in my position once who had grown up and survived the Arena. But I did not take him for a fighter.

If he had a name, he did not share it. His eyes were blank and empty. Despite that, he had overwhelming patience for the children.

21

He brought us hard bread and water. He moistened the bread for those too young to chew and dabbed it at their lips. Somehow, that was enough to prevent starvation.

I remained in those dungeons for five years. I never spoke. I did not see the sun. I just watched, listened, and *waited*.

I saw Three-Grin once every other month. He would come down to the dungeons reeking of beer and piss. He would take stock of his property, point to one of the older slaves, and walk away. In the days that followed, the child he picked would simply disappear.

Sometimes, Three-Grin came down in a blind rage. He would have a sword in one hand and a cudgel in the other. At random he would pick one of the children. Usually it was the one who screamed the most.

Three-Grin could not abide screaming.

He would kick the child to the center of the room. He liked making a spectacle of things. He would impale his sword through the crying child's shoulder, pinning him to the ground. Then he would laugh, and, using the cudgel, beat the poor child into a bloody pulp.

Then he would spin round and round and scream as his crazed eyes found us in the shadows. *"Xune knows all! Xune punishes sinners! Hear me, for I am the great God Xune's one true messenger!"*

He did not know how right he was. Xune was watching. And Xune was preparing to punish sinners.

After Three-Grin left, our robed caregiver would kneel beside the broken body of the latest sacrifice. He would cradle the child's head and hum a haunting melody into one unhearing ear.

It dawned on me later that perhaps the robed man was a disgraced priest. Many worshipped Xune in their own ways. The Church did not have the same influence back then that it does now. But they were growing, and the lies of the religions were spreading like fleas on a ship.

But I digress. Over the years, the Church has been both a great enemy to me and a steadfast friend. I will get to that at its proper time.

Some months after my sixth birthday, I was selected by Three-Grin on one of his patrols. To say I slept poorly that night would be a lie. I did not sleep at all.

Yet it was not fear that kept me awake. It was hope. Being selected was the only way out of the dungeons. I had had enough of that dank place.

Let me remind you that, until that day, I had not heard a human language spoken since my time with the gypsies. Three-Grin's rhetoric did not count. My mind was fallow and ready to absorb anything it could as easily as a sponge.

So, in the night, when I was cloaked, bagged, and abducted from my spot against the wall, I felt the primitive bloom of joy spread through my chest. I did not know what happened to children who were taken in the night. Anticipation trembled in me like a coiled spring.

I was brought up one flight of stairs and dumped to the floor.

That was it. One storey up. It was another dungeon, slightly larger, and right above my previous one.

But even that could not hamper my excitement. My world had just doubled in size. I was overjoyed.

Until somebody drenched me with a bucket of ice cold water from behind.

I gasped and shot up. Two coarse, rough hands grabbed my arms. Instinct told me to fight, but my frozen muscles did not respond. I was picked up and tossed into a tub of steaming water as easily as a ham.

Do you know the pain that comes when you follow a hot mug of *Kaf* with a shot of rum that has been chilled in the snow? The pain that makes your teeth feel like shattering?

That was the pain I knew then, except an order of magnitude stronger. It consumed my entire body. I opened my mouth to scream. Before a single sound could come out, that rough hand found my hair and shoved my head underwater.

I flailed as the deadly liquid filled my lungs. I was drowning. I knew, in the most primitive way possible, that it was my turn to die.

But death was not yet in the cards for me. It still isn't, in fact. Though Xune knows I have tried to seek it out.

I was brought back to the surface. Those rough heavy hands turned me around. I saw my tormenter for the first time.

It was a girl.

No. Saying it that way does not do justice to the surprise I felt. She was not just a girl. She was a beautiful girl. Her bright green eyes seemed to shine in the dim light. Her hair was the color of daffodils. It fell around her face in lush, cascading waves. She smelled sweet, like vanilla with the faintest hint of honey. She had a perfect rosebud mouth, a tiny, delicate nose, and the longest eyelashes I have ever seen.

She was an illusion. A specter. She could not be real.

With no words to guide my thoughts, my mind struggled to understand what someone so beautiful was doing here.

Then she grinned, and dunked me in the tank again.

I sputtered and coughed and gulped down air every time she brought me back to the surface. I still thought I was going to die. But it comforted me to know that I would die at the hands of an angel.

The waterboarding stopped. She picked me up and flung me on a table. When I saw her raise a knife, I got a discomforting sense of *Deja-vu*.

I did not scream or cry. I simply stared at her, transfixed by her beauty. It astounded me how someone with a face so fair could treat another human with such cruelty.

She raised the knife. I closed my eyes. I wanted my last memory of her to be unmarred by fright.

She brought the knife down and chopped off my long, dirty hair.

I blinked, stunned.

And then, I started to scream.

You cannot understand the shock I felt. The betrayal. My hair had never been cut. I thought of it as an essential part of me, as important as any of my limbs or my fingers or—

"Or your penis!" Earl roared, laughing. "What do you say to that, eh? Not a single word in that little brain of yours, but already you're thinking about gettin' yer pecker wet!" He beamed at Patch, who was starting to turn a bright red.

"No," Dagan said. "My love for her was pure. I cherished it and held it tight for years after. It was not twisted by lust. Not yet."

Earl noticed the growing color in Patch's cheeks. "What's wrong with you, lad? You never seen the upside of a woman's skirts?" He exploded into another bout of choppy laughter.

Path glued his eyes to the floor and burned bright.

"Earl." Dagan's voice cut through the man's laughter like a spear through a dying boar. "Look."

Earl stopped and took note of Patch for the first time. He saw the way he drew in on himself. He saw his untouched mug of ale on the table.

He saw the boy's innocence.

"Ahh, lad," he said. "I'm sorry. I didn't know—" he broke off with a cough, "—I mean, I didn't expect you to be, uh…" he snuck a glance at Dagan, suppressed a shiver, and changed what he was going to say. "I didn't expect you to be *so young*. I forget, sometimes, how few summers you've really seen. It's a testament to yer… ahhh… maturity."

Patch's eyes shot up. They burned with a deep but furious flame. "I'm *not* unsullied," he retorted. "I've just got more respect than you. That's all."

Suddenly his eyes widened, and he seemed to remember his company. "I interrupted your story," he said to Dagan, abashedly.

"Perhaps it's time for us to hear yours," Dagan suggested, not unkindly. "Who was she?"

Patch looked down again, uncomfortable being the center of attention. "Nobody," he muttered.

"Ah, lad, come now, we won't tease," Earl said. "My first love was named Lysa. Fair as the wind, she was, and as spirited as the wildest mare. It took me five long years to get her to warm up to me. But I didn't give up."

"Five *years*?" Patch asked in wonder. He could not fathom Earl waiting for someone that long.

"Aye, five years. And let me tell you, it was worth it in the end. Five years is what it took to get one night together."

"And… after?"

"The next day, her husband found out she had left in the night. He beat her. He beat her until she couldn't crawl, then locked her in a room and let her die." Earl's voice hardened. "When I found out why she did not come and see me again, I broke out in a wild rage. I killed the bastard with my own hands. Wrung his neck like a duck's."

"When?" Patch's voice came out as a whisper.

"Forty years ago, maybe more? I vowed, on Lysa's grave, that I would never love another woman the way I loved her. That's why I am the way I am, lad. So, don't be taking offence to the things I say on account of me. They're not meant t'be malicious." He pronounced it *maleeshus*.

"Your turn, now," Dagan reminded Patch gently.

Patch picked up his mug and took his first swallow. He set it down and spoke fast.

"Her name was Eleanor. She grew up beside me on the farm next to my Da's. Well, the farm that used to be my Da's. When the soldiers came looking for recruits, she hid me in her basement. She was a year older than me. The soldiers took my Da."

Patch blinked once and continued. "Four months later, they came back. I hid again. But, they found me. I never saw her since. She promised she would wait for me…" He trailed off and peered into his mug. "That was two years ago."

"Two years ain't nothing," Earl said, seeing the boy's sadness and trying to comfort him. "If she thinks of you th'way you speak of her, she'll be there when you come back."

"Whoever said I was coming back?" Patch whispered.

A silence fell upon the three men. It was a silence like the one that comes after the headman's axe has fallen. It was a silence like the hollow ring of an empty barrel.

It was a silence like death.

Dagan broke it. The silence did not bother him, just as death did not bother him. He had seen death coming for him so often that it provided him familiar comfort by now, like an old friend or lover.

He knew it would come for him once more tonight.

"So," he said, "how about the rest of my story?"

CHAPTER THREE

When I lost my hair, something broke inside me. I screamed. I screamed in sorrow. I screamed in pain. I screamed for all the time I had kept quiet in the dungeon.

The girl smiled. She picked me up and brought me to her breast. She rocked me as the screams turned into sobs. She rocked me until my throat was pained and raw.

Then, she set me down, kissed my forehead, and left.

***

I did not find out who she was until three months later. In the interim, I was treated to varying degrees of torture by a trio of small, masked men. One wore the mask of a hyena. The other, a pig. The last, a wolf.

I was flogged. I was beaten. I was thrown into a fire and then doused with sawdust to stop the flames.

I didn't know it then, but all of that treatment was done to prepare me for the Arena.

Let me paint a picture of my captivity so that you might better understand my struggle. Whereas before, in the dungeon beneath this one, I was merely forgotten, now, I was a target.

I was also somewhat of an enigma.

No matter what the masked men did to me, I did not make a sound. It was almost like I had exhausted my capacity for it the day my hair was cut.

That made my captors curious. Could I not feel pain? Was I immune to their torture devices?

I think it took less than twelve hours for them to make a game of it. The one who would make me scream first would win. Their torture became more and more elaborate. It became more and more creative.

You have to understand one thing about Three-Grin's men. They were there only to train me for the Arena. Anything that would put me at a disadvantage was off-limits.

They would not break my bones. They would not blind my eyes. All they did, and all they were supposed to do, was acclimate my body to pain.

For if I embraced pain—if I could endure it—I might survive the Arena long enough for Three-Grin to make a small fortune on me as a fighter.

So, after they flogged me, they applied balm to my wounds so my skin would heal. After they beat me, they gave me nectar of Red Clover so I might sleep. And after they threw me into the fire...

Well, let's just say that miscalculation nearly cost them their lives.

The girl who cut my hair entered the room just as the man in the pig mask was carrying me, smoldering, from the altar. She gave a horrified gasp and sprang forward. She opened her mouth. Sound came out.

Immediately, the three men prostrated themselves on the floor.

That was the first time I witnessed real magic.

It fascinated me. What would possess three strong men to cower before a little girl? Her mouth kept moving. More sounds came. Some were harsh. But most were smooth and soft, like warm honey.

The soft ones scared the men most.

Instinctively, every person knows what language is. It is hardwired into our brains. Since I had not been exposed to language before, those mystical noises attracted me. They beckoned me like a black-veiled siren in the night. I knew that, somewhere inside, I had the capacity to do the same thing the girl was doing.

So I tried. I parted my lips, touched my tongue to the roof of my mouth, and used my forgotten vocal cords for the first time.

"Faarkher. Faaaarkher."

My angel spun toward me. Her eyes were wide.

"Faarghur," I kept trying. I was repeating the word I heard her use most often. "Faarrkhur. Farghur. Fugher. Fuc—"

She picked me up. "Shh, shh," she cooed in my ear. My body quivered in ecstasy from her touch. She stroked my hair. "Shh, don't say that. Can you walk?" She made a waddling motion.

On some level, I understood her. I nodded and smiled widely, then showed her what I could do.

I stood on my own two feet and backed away, then mimicked that awkward waddle.

She laughed with delight and clapped her hands. Even I was not so far removed from humanity that I could not understand encouragement. I made a show of it for her, stomping my feet against the floor with abandon, making big circles round and round.

She stood up and took my hand. The warmth I felt through that connection was... well, it was unlike anything I'd felt before. It flowed up my arm and made my insides tingle. All of the hurt I had not allowed my body to feel crashed into me. My senses awakened.

I staggered, but did not fall. I satiated in the pain, because feeling it meant that I could feel *her*.

Her hand was still rough and callous, just as before. That did not take away from my pleasure.

She walked with me back to the three men. She barked something at them. I do not remember the words, though I wish I could. They must have been pure brilliance, for they made the three men bury their faces even deeper in the dirt.

The next time I saw any of them, they were bound to an upright log beside a roaring fire. They were being flayed alive.

She took me past the men and up a flight of stairs. There, she unlocked a rough, wooden door. We walked down a long tunnel lit by hanging candles at either end. We passed through another door, and climbed one more flight of stairs. Suddenly, we were home.

Home. How can I describe the countless connotations that that word brings? Home is the place you feel safe. Home is the place you are warm. Home is a person's sanctuary, his retreat from the world.

The place I found challenged all those assumptions.

It was the lower floor of a palace. Rich tapestries hung from the walls. Gleaming tiles decorated the floor. Windows, monstrous windows, brought in the glorious sunlight.

I took my first step forward, and the illusion shattered.

I heard the screams of tortured men and women. They echoed through the halls, not loud enough to be distracting—if you were used to them—but ever-present, and never-ending. When I looked again at the tapestries on the walls, I saw depictions of bloody orgies. Fingers, limbs, and sometimes entire heads were missing from the bodies.

The floor tiles were bright red. They reminded me of blood.

My angel did not seem to mind. I was uncomfortable, but, pride being a prickly thing, did not let it show.

It was the first time I had to pretend for a lady.

We walked down the high-ceilinged, empty hall. We passed a few closed doors. Sometimes, when we did, the screams became louder. Other times, they stayed the same.

I think it obvious I preferred the latter doors.

I was led into the kitchen and sat on a stool. The unnamed girl poured me a bowl of soup. She put it on the table and pushed it toward me.

I did not know what to do.

"Eat," she said, making the appropriate motions. "Eat. Mmm, good. Yum, yum."

"Young yam," I said, smiling. She giggled. I liked her.

I dipped my spoon in the soup and took a mouthful.

My palette exploded in a euphoria of previously unbeknownst tastes. In fact, I was so absorbed in all the new feelings coming to life inside my mouth that I did not notice the entrance of a third person until he was right on us.

My eyes bulged when I saw Three-Grin. He towered over the table like an icy mountain. He looked livid.

He raised an arm to strike me. Before I could do anything, the girl darted in front of me to take the brunt of the blow. Momentary shock rippled across Three-Grin's features.

It had nothing on the shock that I felt.

The girl crumpled to the floor. As she tried to right herself, Three-Grin drove his boot into the small of her back. She gave a tight cry of pain.

The little sound sparked such a fire in me that even I was amazed at my reaction. I flew from the stool and attacked Three-Grin. Biting, clawing, scratching—doing everything I could to hurt the man who was harming my savior.

It was a valiant effort, but in vain. Three-Grin picked me up by the scruff of my neck and threw me against a wall. He did not so much as blink at the effort. He just laughed.

My head bounced off the stone. I saw white stars and felt pain. All the nerves I had so expertly numbed were now sharp as knives.

That meant that I felt every single kick Three-Grin started directing at me ten-fold.

He did not beat me long. Even as he was hitting me, even as I cried out—I had to now, for my shell was broken—I cared only for one thing: the small girl lying on the floor.

My eyes betrayed me.

Three-Grin noticed me looking. His mouth curled up in a crude facsimile of a smile. It emphasized the hideous scars on his cheeks.

He picked me up, reached behind him for some rope, and tied me to the back of a chair.

Don't get me wrong. I struggled against the bonds. I thrashed and flailed and kicked and did everything in my power to break free. But there is only so much a boy of six can do against a grown man.

Three-Grin positioned me so that I would have the perfect view. He turned on the girl—and kicked her hard in the belly.

She gasped. I cried out. Three-Grin looked at me and laughed. I flailed harder. He began hollering at the girl as he landed kicks on her body. She cried and curled into herself.

I screamed.

I screamed with rage and hatred. I screamed because there was nothing else I could do.

I did not hate Three-Grin before. He was simply a constant in my life, doing what he did for reasons unknown to me. But he treated all the children the same, and in the dark, we were anonymous.

Now, he was hurting the first person who showed me kindness. I hated him for it. I screamed, and he took delight in the sound.

As the girl lay whimpering on the floor, Three-Grin picked her up and threw her on the table. I saw the wetness on her face. I hated him all the more for it. He looked at me with a crazed madness, satiating in my pathetic struggle. He reveled in his display of power.

Then, he tore the girl's clothes off.

Her body was a mess of healing, yellow bruises. Welts lined her shoulders and her upper arms. They were old scars, and older half-healed injuries.

I had never seen a creature more beautiful—nor one more to be pitied.

Three-Grin began to rape her.

She did not fight. She could not. I saw the light in her eyes go out. A dull lifelessness came over her as she retreated to some far corner in her mind. Three-Grin growled and pounded into her with an animal ferocity.

She took it without protest.

It was the most horrifying scene I had ever witnessed. When he was done, he splattered his seed all over her belly, then turned and left without so much as a glance at either of us.

A silence grew, broken only by the girl's labored breathing. It was punctuated every once in a while by a short, involuntary whimper.

I possessed no words. But, at that moment, I made a silent vow to kill Three-Grin one day.

Eventually, the girl picked herself up. She shook as she used the tattered clothes to cover her body. Then, without a word, she untied me and brought me to her room.

CHAPTER FOUR

Her name was Alicia, as I learned some months later. She was one of Three-Grin's daughters. She was also his youngest wife.

I adored her. I trailed her everywhere like a shadow.

She taught me to speak. She gave me food. She showed me all the hiding places I could go when I heard Three-Grin approaching.

I did not want to hide. I wanted to fight. But, I was too small.

I hated my body for it.

Alicia endured nightly rapes by her father. I witnessed every single one from behind the wallboards of her closet. She did not fight back once. I could not understand why.

She kept knives in her drawers. She showed them to me. Surely, it would not be hard to hide one under her pillow and use it to slit Three-Grin's throat when he fell asleep beside her, exhausted by his victory?

But Alicia did no such thing. Three-Grin was a monster, and yet she still found it in her heart to forgive him

It was only years after I left that I understood it was not kindness that spared Three-Grin's life.

It was terror.

As I said before, I watched the three masked men be flayed alive. Alicia was not the one to order it. Her father was. He was punishing them for letting me escape.

Weeks passed. I hid when Three-Grin came, and comforted Alicia as best I could when he left. As weeks turned to months, I assumed that her father had simply forgotten about me.

How wrong I was.

***

About a year into my stay with Alicia, I was woken up by the thunderous sound of a crashing door. I jolted upright and, pressing my eye to the crack that let me see into her room, found Three-Grin heaving at the door, his face a red mask of rage.

"Where is he?" he demanded. "Where is the blasted urchin you adopted as your own?"

Alicia rose from bed smoothly. She did not bother tying her robe. She knew that would only anger Three-Grin more.

She faced him head-on and asked, "Who, Father?"

"Whore!" he screamed. He backhanded her against the face, sending her to the floor. Her lower lip burst open. Blood trickled down her chin.

Alicia picked herself up. She took Three-Grin's hand. "Father, pl—"

Three-Grin hit her again. "Whore!" he yelled. "Ungrateful whore! Lying bitch! I know you're sheltering him, so WHERE IS HE?"

Alicia started to shake. She did not answer. She would not betray me.

Three-Grin picked her up and threw her over the bed. He grabbed her hair and shoved her head into the mattress. Then he started fiddling with his belt.

I couldn't take it anymore. This was my opportunity to strike. Three-Grin's back was toward me. The drawer of knives stood between me and him.

I burst from the closet in a flash. I was underfed, but that made me light, and quick. I reached the drawer in a tenth of a second. Another half a breath, and I leapt forward, blade in hand, aiming it straight at Three-Grin's neck.

The man moved with such sinuous speed that I could never have expected it from one his size.

He twisted back. One hand knocked the knife from my fingers. The other curled into a fist and caught me right in the stomach.

The punch drove the air out of my lungs. I fell and hit the floor hard. Before I could so much as cough, Three-Grin landed on top of me.

He reeked of sweat and stale beer. His short, curling hair clumped around his temples. His eyes burned with bloodlust.

"No!" Alicia screamed. "No, Father! Let him go!"

Three-Grin ignored his wailing daughter. He looked down at me and spoke. "I hear the Arena calling your name, boy. I've fed and housed you for too long. It's time you repay what you owe."

Alicia's screams continued in the background. Three-Grin turned his head and yelled, "Shut up!"

He punctuated his request by picking up my knife and casually flinging it at her.

Time slowed as I watched the blade arc through the air. Alicia had only a second to widen her eyes.

Then the sharp metal point sunk into her throat.

She made a wet, gurgling sound and fell to her knees. I watched, horrified, as her hands desperately tried to stem the blood flow.

They did not so much as reach halfway. She toppled forward, dead.

My hatred for the man exploded in a furious inferno of flame.

I went feral. I scratched and clawed and bit. I did everything I could to break free from under Three-Grin's body.

It was all wasted effort.

He grabbed my hair and twisted my neck toward the body of my angel. He brought his face close to mine.

"You see her?" he snarled. "She's dead because of you. *You* did that to her. Look. LOOK!"

I looked. I saw the shape of the poor, fallen girl. I saw the blood pulsing out of her neck with the final beats of her heart. I saw the red stain crawl up the white fabric of her robe.

Most of all, I saw my failure to protect her.

"Remember that image," Three-grin breathed. "Remember what you caused. Remember, when you're fighting in the Arena. Remember Xune. Remember that He punishes all sinners. Remember that Xune alone sees your guilt."

He picked my head up and slammed it against the floor. I blacked out.

CHAPTER FIVE

I came to with a searing pain behind my eyelids. My entire body hurt.

I groaned and rolled over. For a moment, I debated never opening my eyes and simply sinking into the darkness.

Then I remembered Alicia.

My eyes popped open. I jerked up. And was greeted by a sight never seen before.

I was in the back of a cart pulled by a team of mules. I was behind bars, and I was not alone.

There were nine other cages around mine. Each held a small child. Most were scrawny, pathetic things. I reckoned I was the oldest.

A man with long, white hair sat at the front, directing the animals. He was humming a song I had never heard before.

Then again, I had not heard any songs before.

The cart bumped and lurched along a dirt road. I looked around. We were in a forest. Rays of sunlight pierced the green foliage. For a boy who had never been in the woods before, it was a magical sight.

I noticed that the child in the cage across from mine was also awake. He huddled back, rocking on his heels. His eyes were wide and owlish, as if he expected someone to hit him at any moment.

"Hey!" I hissed. "Psst! Hey, you! Where are we?"

The boy looked at me in absolute terror. He started rocking faster.

"Psst! Hey! Where are we going?"

The boy clamped his hands over his ears and started moaning.

Then it hit me: He couldn't speak.

He was one of Three-Grin's slave children, raised only for the Arena. Except that the treatment I received seemed to have broken him.

I saw movement from out of the corner of my eye. I looked over, and ducked just in time to avoid being hit by a rotting apple thrown at my head.

The white-haired man in the front had a companion. Apparently, he'd been sleeping before, hidden from view by the back of the seats.

He was short. Ugly red pimples covered his face. His small, beady eyes reminded me of a rat's. And he seemed to take sport of tormenting the children.

He threw another apple at me. This one hit the bar of my cage and splattered sickly-sweet juices over my face. The small man laughed.

The white-haired driver looked over. "What the hell are you doing, Karl?" he asked. He saw the small man hefting another rotten fruit, and caught his arm before he could throw. "Idiot! Those are for selling in the city, not for throwing away like trash!"

"What city?" I asked.

My voice startled the men. They both jerked their heads toward me. Karl's jaw dropped open. The older man simply stared.

The moment seemed to last a decade. It was the first time I was acknowledged by someone other than Alicia or Three-Grin.

The white-haired man pulled on the reins and stopped the cart. The other one hopped into the back and peered down at me over his belly.

"Well, well," the old man said. "We've got us a talker. Been a long time since Three-Grin's given us a talker, hasn't it, Karl?"

The short man grunted in reply.

The white-haired man climbed out of his seat and came up to my side of the cart. Our eyes were on the same level. "What's your name, boy?"

"Dagan," I said. That was the name Alicia had given me.

"Dagan, eh? A good, strong name. How old are you, Dagan?"

"I don't know."

He chuckled. "You don't know? Now, how does a smart young man like you go about not knowin' his own age?"

I looked around at the forest. "I've never been outside," I said.

The old man seemed shocked. For a moment, I thought he was genuine. "You've never been outside," he muttered, shaking his head. He gestured around at the woods. "Well, welcome to the great, big world, then."

"Say," Karl said from behind me. I turned toward his voice. "The kid looks hungry. Are you hungry, Dagan?" He produced a shiny red apple from out of his sleeve. He held it out to me. "Would you like a bite?"

I was starving. The provisions Alicia had managed to sneak to me were getting smaller and smaller each week. Or perhaps they only seemed that way because I was growing. I didn't know how long I'd been in the cage, either, so I had no idea when my last meal had been.

But I was also cautious. Something about the offer did not feel right. Kindness and generosity were not things in abundance in my world.

I didn't answer.

The short man squatted down. He brought the apple to his mouth and took a large bite. Juices leaked down his chin.

"It's sweet," he said, showing me the mulch in his mouth. A small piece of apple stuck to his whiskers. "You sure you don't want some?"

"Maybe he's thirsty, Karl," the other man cackled from behind me. "Would you like a drink, boy?"

Even the cruelest slaver had to give his property water. I was parched. "Yes," I answered.

The sound of Karl rising behind me was all the warning I got. He took out his cock and started urinating on my head.

I was drenched in hot, stinking piss.

Let me say this. If my stay with Alicia taught me one thing, it was the importance of appearances. Her father beat her. He raped her. In her rooms, she allowed herself to cry.

But the moment she stepped over the threshold of her door, she became as regal as a queen. People feared her because she was Three-Grin's wife. She allowed them to see her only as such.

That was the true power behind the words she spoke to my three masked tormentors on the day she rescued me. They feared Three-Grin. By extension, they feared her.

So, I did not cower, or sputter, or shy back from the stream. These men could try to humiliate me. But they would not see me afraid.

Karl laughed as he shook out the last few drops. The older man hit the cage, rattling it. He got my attention.

"That's what we do to talkers, boy. So, keep yer mouth shut. If I hear so much as a whimper from you again, it won't be piss landing on your head next time."

"And have your Goddamned bite," Karl added. He took a mouthful of apple, chewed it up, and spat it at me.

I spent the rest of the day cold, hungry, and reeking of urea.

CHAPTER SIX

The cart stopped for the night in the middle of an abandoned field. There was a crumbling farmhouse to one side. We'd left the forest together with the setting sun, and have been continuing over flat, grassy land for last few hours.

Not once along our journey did we see another soul. Because of that, I started to think we were the only people left in the world.

The other children got their provisions of bread and water. I was told the gifts Karl bestowed upon me earlier that day would suffice.

The two men started a fire. They deliberately positioned the cart far away so that we would not feel any of the warmth.

They drank and smoke and ate. They told stories to each other and laughed. They drank some more, until the embers of the fire were the only things left aglow. Then they fell asleep, and we continued on in the morning.

I spent ten days in the back of that cart. Ten days where I could not stand or stretch my legs. Ten days where I was forced to shit in the corner of my cage like all the other children.

On the eleventh day, things became interesting.

We'd stopped early for the evening. I heard the men talking about the mules getting tired and needing to give them a break. They treated the animals better than they did us.

The white-haired man started tending the mules, while Karl went to start a fire. I anticipated another ten hours spent shivering in the cold. At least it wasn't raining.

But then my ears picked up a distant sound. It was like a low rumble that came from the earth. Karl and the white-haired man were too preoccupied to notice. The other children did not care.

I turned my head toward it. It was coming from the side of the road we had not gone down yet. It was getting louder. It sounded like trampling feet.

The two men both heard it at the same time. The old man cursed. He rushed to get a canvas from the back and throw it over the cages. It landed crooked and did not fully cover mine.

By then, the sound of men and horses was too distinct to remain unknown. While I knew better than to expect a rescue, my heart still swelled with the hope of seeing other people.

You might think that I should have felt scared. But, I had already suffered the cruelty of torture. I had watched as the only person I cared about—and the only who cared about me—choked and died on her own blood. I had been beaten, burned, and pissed on.

In short, there was little I feared from men anymore.

So I watched, fascinated, as a cavalry of riders barreled past us on the road. They did not spare a single glance in our direction.

They were tall. They wore silver swords over their backs. Their armor shone white in the dying light. They sat straight and proud, with their heads held high. They were defiant.

I would later learn the riders I saw were named the Knights of Valamor. They and I have history. I will get to that at its proper time.

It would not be a stretch to say that, at that moment, I did not know much of the world. But even I could tell the sight of the riders unnerved the old man with the beard.

"Noble pigs," he spat after the last of them was out of earshot. "No better than cowards, the way they always group together. I tell ya, the moment I find one of them alone, I'll—"

He did not get to finish his threat. An arrow fell from the sky like a diving bird and struck him in the middle of the forehead.

For a second, he just stood there, too stunned to move. It was as if his body was slow telling him that he was dead.

Then, he fell to the ground like an upended sack of potatoes.

Shadows started to move.

More accurately, *shapes* started to move in the shadows. A small army of foes had gathered around us while Karl and the now-dead man were distracted by the riders.

I saw a hundred pairs of eyes encroach upon the cart in a silent circle.

Karl looked around in fright. He took out his sword and held it in one shaking hand.

"Who goes there?" he cried out. An arrow hissed by his ear. "Show yourself!"

A man stepped forward from the rest. His face was veiled. Black, tattered robes hung off his body like dark smoke.

His clothes were deceptive. They were not the shabby scraps of a beggar. They were the garb of a killer, and they hid him well in the night.

Karl tried to make himself tall as he faced the man. His round bulk and poor coordination made the attempt laughable.

He looked around, trying to get a count of his enemies. But I knew he would never fight. He was craven.

"W-what do you want?" he stammered. He pointed his sword at the neck of the tall, masked man. "Stay back. I-I'm warning you, s-s-stay back!"

The man raised one hand. I heard a rush of air, as if the very earth had just released a long-held breath. The tall man's companions all rose from their crouched positions by the ground.

I was wrong before. They were not one hundred. They were not even ten.

"Peace, friend," the tall man spoke. He had a strange, lulling accent. His speech was not of the common tongue. "We are not here to harm you."

"You killed John!" Karl accused, glancing back at the body of his friend. "You killed John in cold blood!"

"Lay down your sword, and we will not touch you."

"A-a truce?" Karl asked. He nodded. "Yes. Yes. Okay. Okay, I will—

"NO!" he roared. He gripped his sword harder. "Why would I trust you? I've heard of you savages! The minute I drop my weapon, you'll gut me like a pig!"

"It is not you we want," the tall man said. He looked past Karl. His eyes met mine. "It is him."

For a second, my vision faded from shock. I could not believe my ears. What use could I be to them? *Who* were they?

Karl looked over his shoulder. I saw his face. It was the pale face of a man who knew he was already dead.

"T-the kid?" he sputtered. "Take him. Take them all! Just please, spare me."

"We will," the leader answered, "if you drop your sword."

Karl looked around. I could almost see the wheels turning in that pimply head of his. He was outnumbered now, just the same as before. He could not fight. But, if he surrendered…

"O-okay." Karl eased his grip on the sword. "Okay, I'll do it. H-here. N-nice and slow now, a-a-all right?"

He bent forward. The tip of his sword touched the ground. He let the hilt roll out of his fingers.

"There," he said, standing up. "T-there. Okay? I did what you said. N-now, you promised to let me go."

"I did," the tall man nodded. Casually, he reached over his shoulder and nocked an arrow.

Then, he aimed it at Karl.

"Run, fat man," he whispered.

A space cleared behind Karl. He looked around wildly, unsure of what to do…

"I said," the man repeated, "*run*."

Karl ran. He ran as fast as his short, stubby legs would carry him. He ran into the night, gasping and squelching as he sucked in air. He ran until I could no longer see his shape in the dark.

"*Now*," the tall man breathed. He released his arrow. For a moment, all was silent save for the reverberation of his string.

Then I heard a dull, wet *thud*. Karl made one dying choke as he fell to the dirt.

The man and his companions turned their attention to the cart. Two of them cut the mules loose and sent them running with a sharp slap on their hindquarters. Another pulled the canvas off. It rippled to the ground.

The tall man nudged John's cold body as he approached. "Human traffickers," he muttered. "Scum of the earth."

I heard hoof beats in the distance.

"They're coming, m'lord," one of the veiled men announced.

"Yes. I can hear them." He raised his voice. "Break open the cages. Free all the children! Offer them the same choice I gave you."

Sounds exploded around me as his subordinates went to work. The cart rocked as they pulled all the cages off and splintered open the doors with swords and axes.

All, that is, except for mine.

"Not you," the leader said, stepping toward me. "I have a special place for you."

My small hands gripped the bars of my cage as I stared at him, trying to understand who he was. I felt no fear. But I did feel an extreme curiosity.

He looked me over in silence. His eyes swept over my small and dirty body.

"By Xune," he muttered, "you are him, aren't you?" He reached out and put his hand through the cage. He touched my collarbone where my mother's blade left a scar.

I did not flinch away.

"Can you speak?" he asked. "Do you know my language?" He changed his inflection. "*Apritti? Honlart apritti?*" Another tonal shift. "*Exl'rar? Rak'r mor exl'tgri?*"

"I know your language," I said.

The man sucked in a quick breath. "Xune be praised," he whispered. He turned to one of the men beside him. "Simenon! See this one free. Be on your guard, man, but do it!"

His companion turned toward me. I looked at him. Our eyes met.

For half a heartbeat, he seemed to falter.

Then he raised his axe and swung it down onto the crude chain that served as my lock.

It splintered under the heavy blow. I tried the door. The hinges creaked as it opened.

By now, the sound of hoof beats was impossible to ignore. I looked back and saw the riders returning.

The tall man took me by the shoulders and lifted me from the cart. He set me down and knelt to my level.

"They come for you," he said gravely. "But they do not yet know what you look like." His fingers touched the dirt, and he spread two lines of it on either side of my nose. Then, he pressed something round and hard into my hand.

"Take this. Do not lose it. Treasure it with your life. When the time comes, I will find you again."

He straightened and looked at the approaching knights. "Go! Any direction away from the road. When the sun rises tomorrow, walk toward it. You will find the city of Hallengard. Enter in broad daylight. Avoid the alleys. Stay close to people on the main road. Follow the path until you see a grand structure in the heart of the city. It is a building unlike any other. The road splits two ways around it.

"Go up the steps. Show the first person inside what I gave you. You will be cared for."

He looked up. The riders were getting closer. He pushed my shoulders in one direction. "Go now! We will distract them for you. Go!"

Another push sent me into a lurching run. I squeezed my fingers around whatever it was I held in my hand, afraid to look at it for fear of dropping it.

I ran.

My leg muscles screamed at me as I worked them. I saw a great flash of light, felt a blaze of heat, and turned my head just in time to see the cart go up in flames. The conflagration roared in the night.

Chapter Seven

I ran until my legs could no longer carry me. By then, the fire was just a small flickering light in the distance. I could hardly believe I was still alive.

I saw what had happened to Karl when he ran. I half expected the same fate. But when I passed his body, face down on the ground, and my insides tensed in anticipation… and when the arrow didn't come… I thought that perhaps the man who had freed me had told me the truth.

I ran much farther than that. My ankle betrayed me first. I stepped into a ditch, my foot twisted, and I yelped out in pain as I fell to the ground.

My lungs cried for air but I didn't breathe. I strained my ears for any sound of pursuit.

There was none.

Still, I crawled farther. I crawled until my hands were bloody and sore. I crawled until I sapped every last bit of strength from my failing body.

I crawled until I reached a tree. Then, tired, achy, and absolutely exhausted, I fell into my first slumber as a free man.

***

I woke late, with the sun high overhead, and panicked when I had no idea where to go.

Then I noticed the shadow cast by the tree. I crawled out and traced its outline in the dirt. I waited, and did it again. Using what could only be referred to as common sense, I discovered the journey of the sun in the sky, and set out in the opposite direction.

It was a slow, laborious process. My ankle was swollen and hot to the touch. I could barely walk. My limp made things very awkward.

In the light, I discovered that the object the man had given me was a coin. As I walked, I kept trailing my thumb over the raised surface.

It depicted a wooden cross with a body hanging from it. Flames licked up the corpse's legs. The other side had a flowing script in letters I could not read.

The coin had become the single most important thing in my life. For, though I lost it later, when I retrieved it again, it helped define the man I would become.

***

"And here it is," Dagan said, placing his fist on the table with a solid *thud*. "The mark of Rel'ghar."

He withdrew his hand slowly, leaving the thick coin in the middle of the tabletop.

Earl choked on his drink as his eyes fell upon it. Patch sucked in a reverent breath.

The young boy reached out, tentatively, eyes darting to Dagan as if to ask for permission. Dagan gave an almost imperceptible nod.

Patch's fingers brushed one cool, smooth edge. A sudden jolt ran up his arm, and he jerked back.

"Great Xune," Earl muttered. His eyes flashed at Patch. "Do you know what that is, boy? Do you know how much that's worth?"

"Viridian gold," Patch answered. "I've heard stories, but I never thought... I never thought that I would see it in my life."

"Hah!" Earl barked. "Say that when you're my age, and then it'll hold real meaning." He looked toward Dagan, narrowly avoiding his eyes. "May I?"

The hooded man gestured him to go ahead almost absently. His thoughts were not on the coin.

He could sense Death coming.

He could feel it as surely as he could feel his right ear. It was not him Death was coming for, but he could feel it nonetheless.

Dagan's eyes lifted from the table for half a breath. That was enough for him to get a count of everybody in the room.

Eight men sat by the bar. Two groups of five gambled in the corners. The barkeeper was watching over them. Dagan knew her three daughters were asleep upstairs.

Twenty-five occupants, counting him and his two companions. How many would die tonight?

He reckoned it would be twenty-four. Twenty-four was a good, even number. Twenty-four was a multiple of three. It meant that the trio of Death's heads would feast on eight throats each.

When Death came, it did not like to leave any of its heads hungry.

Could he save them? Probably. Yet, life's experience had taught him that cheating Death required a tribute equal to those spared.

Did he have it in him to offer the proper sacrifice tonight?

He looked at Patch. The boy was young, and held untapped potential. Perhaps it would be worth it to rescue him tonight. The experience would change the boy forever.

Sometimes, an unexpected mercy could pay dividends later.

Dagan returned his attention to the table. Earl was cradling the coin in the palm of his hand. His arm shook as he brought it over the lip of his mug. He turned his hand slowly. The coin fell away only when his palm was perpendicular to the ground.

It dropped in the warm ale with a hiss. Dagan heard the clink as it hit the metal bottom.

The mug burst into flames.

Earl gasped and jerked back. Patch gripped the sides of the table and brought his head closer.

Fearless, Dagan thought. *A trait that will serve him well in the future.*

He decided, on the spot, that saving Patch would be worthwhile. The boy's potential was too great to waste just yet.

CHAPTER EIGHT

"The mark of Rel'ghar has great history," Dagan began as the flames leapt from the mug. "Let me speak of it now."

Rel'ghar was a nation of great kings and witches. It was an empire that had stood untouched for millennia. Great wars were waged at its walls. Sieges and assaults that lasted years. The most fearsome foes were turned away like waves against a stony shore.

Rel'ghar withstood all.

But, there was one in the city who loathed it. His name was Vontas.

Vontas was the youngest of three brothers, like me. His father ruled Rel'ghar. He was a man strict but fair. The city flourished under his rule. Even as the rest of the world was ravaged by war and famine, Rel'ghar remained proud and untouched.

It was the jewel of the world.

Men, women, and children from the six corners of the world traveled in search of the famed sanctuary. Some spent their entire lives wandering without finding it. Others were killed a day's march from its doors.

But all who made it had one thing in common. They were all pure of heart.

Long before the great city was built, longer still than the time that has passed since its collapse to now, the ground upon which Rel'ghar stood belonged to a coven of witches. Magic was feared and hated back then. The witches hid themselves in a place no one could find in order to preserve their way of life.

But one man did find them. His name was Rel. He had no hatred in his heart for the unnatural forces. He did not fear any of Xune's creatures, because he knew that they were the same as he.

He was not a rich man, nor powerful. He did not own chests of gold or acres of fertile land. His sole belongings consisted of the clothes on his back and the thoughts in his mind.

Rel was a philosopher. He made his way from town to town, from village to village, and spent his days teaching those who would listen. His great desire was to make the mysteries of the mind known to all.

His task was not easy. He found men who were wary of his words. He found enemies. At a time when one cold snap meant the difference between a field full of crops and a slow death by starvation, his teachings were not welcome. They drew people's attention away from the two necessities of life: food, and warmth.

Rel remained in each village for as long as he was permitted. He did not argue or complain when he was chased out. He trusted that the seeds of his words would take root and sprout. If he could show some people, somewhere, that life was more than an empty struggle, he left fulfilled.

The witches noticed his plight. They watched him from their dark place and whispered amongst themselves. "Here is a man unlike the others," they said. "Here is a man we should not fear."

So, little by little, they nudged Rel toward their coven. Bit by bit, they drew him closer. It took thirty long years for him to find them.

By then, Rel was a man old and grey. He had endured the harshness of the world, but it had not changed him. His purpose remained steadfast. His heart remained pure.

When he crossed the threshold to the coven, he fell to his knees and cried in joy. He saw the witches for who they really were: beautiful beings to be respected, not hideous creatures to be feared.

The witches told him to stand. They would not have him bow to them, as they would not bow to him. They considered Rel their sole equal in the world.

They fed and bathed him. They gave him clothes that would strike envy in the hearts of the richest kings. They spoke to him of their crafts, and delighted in his philosophy.

One year passed. Rel grew stronger and younger with each passing day. Such was the gift the witches bestowed upon him.

Yet Angelica, the most powerful of all witches, could not help but notice the growing sadness within Rel's heart.

One day, as they walked arm-in-arm through her gardens, she spoke. "My dear philosopher," she said, "you are carrying a heavy burden. Tell me, what troubles your mind?"

"You have been to kind to me," Rel answered, "and I have no way of paying you back."

"That is not your trouble," Angelica said.

"You have given me everything a man can hope for," Rel answered, "and I have no way of paying you back."

"That is not your trouble," Angelica said.

"You have granted me renewed life and vitality," Rel answered, "and I have no way of paying you back."

"That is not your trouble," Angelica said.

Rel thought on his next words. He knew Angelica could see the true hearts of men. He could not deceive her—even if he so desired.

"My trouble is this," he told her with a sigh. "And I shall only confide it in you. I have seen the wonders of your world. I have seen the power of your magic. But I am not the one who needs it. It is the men who are unlike me that need to witness it, for it shall grant them hope."

"And what good is hope," Angelic asked, "for men who are unworthy?"

"Hope is worth life itself," Rel answered. "Hope is for all kinds of men. Hope is what drives them to build a better future. Hope is what allows men to become worthy."

"The ones you speak of are already condemned," Angelica said. "They are so because of their own choices. They will not change."

"You see the hearts of men, but you pass judgment too easily."

"You are the only one worthy to walk among our coven."

"If that is the true wisdom of your soul," Rel told her, "then cast me out."

Angelica stopped. She turned on him. "You would forsake us?" she asked. "You would turn your back on us, who have given you so much?"

"You have given me the choice of abandoning my people. It is not a choice I can make."

Angelica looked into Rel's heart, and she saw that his words were true. His sincerity troubled her.

"Very well," she said. "I shall not cast you out. Instead, I will let you return to the land you were born. If you come to us with five others—two men, and three women—who have your same purity of heart, they will be allowed to enter.

"But be warned," she added. "If just one of them plays you false, you shall never look upon my face again."

Rel agreed. He ventured back into the world. It took him twenty more years to find five others. But find them he did. When he returned to the coven, Angelica clasped him to her breast and whispered the words that would bind him to her forever, for she was in love.

Rel transformed before her eyes. His back straightened. His hair became a rich brown. He felt the energy return to his body. When he rose, he stood forty years younger.

His five friends saw what Angelica had done. They fell to the ground and praised her mercy. For they knew, deep inside, that Rel's journey had carried him to death's door.

Later that night, in the largest bedchamber of the tallest tower, Angelica and Rel made love. He impregnated her with his child. Nine months later, the first king of Rel'ghar was born.

That is the founding story of the great city. "Ghar" means, "son of." The witches named their coven after the man who brought them back to the world, and their magic protected the walls for many years.

Yet darkness lurks in every man's heart. Of Rel's five friends, one harbored a tiny sliver of evil deep in his soul. It was so small that Angelica chose to overlook it, for she knew Rel could have found none better.

That man wedded one of the women who came with him. Together, they had a daughter. Years later, that daughter married Rel's only son.

The sliver of darkness had wormed its way into the royal line at its inception, where it lay latent for many generations, until finally, in the heart of Vontas, it flared to life.

Continuing the tradition set out by Angelica, the kings of Rel'ghar welcomed all those with a pure heart into their city. They did it to keep darkness out.

Little did they know that darkness had been lurking within them the whole time.

Perhaps things would have been different if Vontas had been the firstborn. Perhaps his thirst for power would have been quenched when he inherited the crown.

But that is not the story that is told today.

Perhaps things would have been different if Vontas had been the second son. Perhaps his thirst for power would have been quenched had he inherited command of the city watch.

But that is not the story that is told today.

For Vontas was the third. Like I, he inherited nothing.

His hatred for Rel'ghar took hold when he and his brothers were still children. His father came into their room and sat them down after they had all turned of age. He told them that Lagon, the oldest, would become King. He told them that Avery, the quickest, would become Commander. And he told them that Vontas, the weakest, would become whoever his brother the king commanded him to be.

That awoke a furious sense of injustice within Vontas. Even as his brothers laughed and told him he would rule with them side by side, he seethed. He seethed with the pure hatred only possible in a spurned ten-year-old boy.

He vowed to himself, that day, that he would kill Lagon and Avery before they inherited rule.

But the darkness had not yet consumed the entirety of Vontas's soul. There was good in him, too. Every time he thought to strike, guilt and remorse stopped him.

Vontas grew into a shell of the man he could have been. He distanced himself from his peers. His inability to act ate away at him as he aged. He hated himself for his cowardice.

His father died the year Vontas turned twenty-five. Lagon inherited the crown. And though Vontas hated Lagon, he was still too frightened to do anything.

Vontas's loathing poisoned his mind. He stayed in his rooms, coming out to see the sun only once a year. He plotted ways to overthrow his brothers as quickly as he discarded them. He spoke to no one. He slept alone.

The only bright spot in his life was the maiden Isabella. She was half his age. He watched her every morning from the window of his chambers as she woke early and helped her father prepare the smithy.

Perhaps if he had gone out and said a word, Isabella's kindness would have subdued the darkness in his heart.

But that is not the story that is told today.

No. Instead, Vontas watched as his brother, Avery, greeted the girl every morning. When she turned fourteen, Avery began courting her. They were married within the year.

The morning of their wedding day, as Isabella was woken up and carried away by her bridesmaids, she looked up at Vontas's window for the first time. Vontas froze as their eyes met. Isabella offered him a shy, sad smile that meant so many things that cannot be described in mere words.

That smile, and the promise of seeing it again, was what finally propelled Vontas to action.

Vontas knew that, if he left the city, he could not return. His true nature would be revealed. But that did not bar him from communicating with those outside.

That night, when the moon was hidden by the clouds, Vontas climbed the city walls. Seeing his brother was the excuse he used for coming up there. In truth, he had written a letter that described Rel'ghar's greatest weakness:

Rel'ghar was not built on magic alone. It owed half its stature to great architectural feats. It was a marvel that showcased the ingenuity of man. A series of aqueducts fed the city water from the highest mountains. They did not run straight into Rel'ghar, but instead stopped some leagues off, where they seemed to have simply collapsed. Water poured over the edge into a deep crater, never to be seen again.

That drop off was part of the design. Underground pipes caught the escaping water and carried it the rest of the way to the city.

None could suspect the secret of the aqueducts or their connection to Rel'ghar. To passersby, they looked like ancient ruins.

But Vontas knew better. He knew, and wrote of the weakness and cast his letter over the side of the wall, to be carried by the dark ocean of the night. He trusted those who hated Rel'ghar as much as he would discover the communication.

Anxious months passed. Isabella moved to live with Avery after their wedding. Vontas never saw her again.

Doubt grew in Vontas's mind. Had he been specific enough? Had he trusted too much in chance?

One night, he was awakened by a raven pecking at his window. He opened the glass and let the bird in. It had a message tied to one foot:

Dear Friend,

Tonight is the night we strike. We wish to thank you. At the hour of our moon's peak, come to the place you spoke of. We will be waiting.

Vontas ran. He ran to the gate where the underground pipes opened to bring water into Rel'ghar. There, he found a great beast cloaked in shadows.

"Open this gate, and let my kin in," the beast said. "Open this gate, and let your revenge be known."

The beast's words shook Vontas. They were not spoken in the common tongue, or in any tongue he knew. Still, through some power of sorcery, he understood.

Vontas threw open the gate and let in the army that would destroy the city.

In minutes, screams pierced the night. Alarm bells rang. The city watchmen ran to their posts, seeking attackers past the walls, not within. They were slaughtered with their backs turned.

The city burned. It burned so bright that the night was cast away by artificial day.

The enemy had a wizard in their ranks, and he hated all witches. Rel'ghar burned from the flames sprouted of the mouth of the dark creature the wizard had summoned out of hell.

By daybreak, none was left alive save Vontas. The culmination of all his desires had come. He stood proudly over the carcass of his brother, the King. He stood proud of the burned remains of his brother, the Commander. And he wept when he found the body of the maiden Isabella.

He wept from joy, not grief. If he could not have her, his hateful heart told him that no other should.

Vontas stood alone as the sole survivor of Rel'ghar, and his weeping transformed into laughter

But the wizard saw the man's true nature. The wizard, like Angelica, could see into the hearts of men. And he saw that Vontas still ached for one thing.

Vontas wanted to be ruler.

He struck Vontas from behind and knocked him down. The wizard and his army had no use for the ruins of Rel'ghar. They had eliminated the spawn of witches. That had been their only purpose.

And Vontas, however unfaithful to the city, was one of Rel'ghar's own.

The armies collected all the gold of Rel'ghar and cast it on the ground. They erected a cross on top, and nailed Vontas's hands and feet to it. The man screamed. His blood poured down and tainted every coin.

"You wanted power," the wizard said, "and now you have it. You wanted revenge, and now you have it. You wanted the city to yourself, and now you have that, too."

The wizard turned to the beast beside him and whispered in his ear. A great gout of flame erupted from the beast's monstrous jaws. It ignited the gold at Vontas's feet.

The wizard cast two spells that day. The first was a spell that would keep Vontas alive until the last ounce of gold had been removed from the city. The second let the beast's fire burn for all eternity.

Those were the last Great Spells that this world has seen.

With the witches and their offspring dead or dying, the wizard had no cause to remain in this world. He took his armies and his beast and disappeared forever.

Vontas's screams endured for two hundred years. They echoed as his blood mixed with the melting gold beneath him.

People all over the world heard of Rel'ghar's downfall. They heard of Vontas's betrayal. And they heard of the treasure burning at his feet. They sought it out.

When the last piece of gold was taken from the ruins of Rel'ghar, the curse was lifted. And to this day, when mothers warn their children of greed and avarice, they speak of Vontas, whose screams still carry on the wind, all these centuries later.

***

"And that," Dagan concluded, "is the story of Vontas and the Marks of Rel'ghar. His treacherous blood poisons each coin, and traces of the wizard's last spell—" he gestured to the melted metal on the table that used to be a mug, "—remain to this day."

"Two hundred years, eh?" Earl grunted. "That's a bloody long time. I wouldn't believe it, if I hadn't seen that mark of yours."

"Two hundred years," Dagan said simply.

"What happened to the rest of the marks?" Patch wondered. "I heard most of them were lost."

"Lost, hoarded, or melted," Dagan agreed. "Only fifty such coins exist in the world today." He swept his off the table and made it disappear. "Of course, when I received mine, people believed there were even fewer..."

CHAPTER NINE

The journey to Hallengard took me three days. It was a journey that an able-bodied man could have made in six hours.

My ankle slowed me. So did my hunger. I could not yet hunt or trap. Survival was an instinct I possessed, but not a skill I could call upon in the open country.

The first day, I found a blackberry bush. I feasted on the small fruits until I was stuffed. It was the first time in my life that consumption did not have a hard limit.

I paid for the binge an hour later by vomiting all over my clothes.

From then on, every time I passed a similar bush, I picked only as many berries as would fit in my hand. I nibbled on them as slowly as I could.

I found the city on the morning of the third day. It rose in the distance, the land around it clear of trees for many leagues. I learned later that this was so enemy armies could not approach unnoticed.

Hallengard was a city build atop a mountain. Its walls seemed to rise as natural outgrowths in the rock. As I got closer, I realized that it had not been erected, but carved.

There was only one road leading through the walls. During the day, it was full of caravans and bustling travelers. I looked at my rags and compared them to what I saw others wearing.

They did not match.

I would stick out the moment I stepped into the crowds. The thought of attracting attention made me nauseous.

But I had no choice other than to keep going. I gripped my mark tightly, and, remembering the words the man in the black had told me, joined the steady stream of people.

.

Relief fell onto my shoulders when I found I was mostly ignored.

If you have never been to Hallengard, allow me to paint a picture for you. It is a city comprised of eighty thousand people. It was built to house a hundred thousand more.

The rich flock to the north of the city. The poor, to the south. That leaves a swath of largely abandoned structures stretching through the middle.

That was the part of Hallengard I found myself in, on my way to the building the stranger told me about, when I was pushed to the ground from behind.

"Well, well, well! Look what we've got here," a surprisingly high-pitched boy's voice chuckled. I began to twist back, but a boot landed on my spine and kept me down. "A little lost wanderer!"

"What's he got there, Duke?" a second voice asked. "Look, in his hand! He's holding suthin'!"

I tried to pull my outstretched hand under my body to protect the mark.

I saw movement from the sides of my vision. A dirty, ragged, little boy, no older than I was, jumped onto my arm and started to pry my fingers open.

My strength was ferocious. The coin was the only thing I had. I would not let it go without a fight.

The boy sank his teeth into my knuckles.

I cried out in pain. My hand opened automatically. The coin bounced over the cobblestone, making metallic clinks as it went.

The boy jumped off and retrieved it. The boot lifted from my back. I scrambled up, and twisted around to see the bullies for the first time.

There were three of them. The oldest, and by far the fattest, was the one who had stepped on me. I took him to be Duke. The other two looked like twins, or at least brothers. It was hard to tell through the dirt caking their faces. They wer

twigs.

Duke was the only one who had clothes without any noicc.

"Whatcha got there?" he called out to the boy who had retrieved my coin.

"It's gold, Duke," he answered. His voice carried an awed inflection.

Duke screwed up his face. "It's not *gold*, you moron," he said. He held out his hand. "Give it here."

The boy walked back, cradling the coin in his cupped hands. He extended it out to Duke.

I pounced.

In retrospect, that was probably not the smartest move. But I had a furious possessiveness of that coin. I saw my chance, and I took it.

atched the coin from Duke's sausagey fingers. A glorious sense of triumph bloomed inside me. I turned and ran.

That triumph disappeared when something hard cracked against the back of my skull.

Pain exploded inside my head. The blow knocked me off balance, and I fell to the ground. I heard laughter around me.

"Stupid, stupid boy," Duke said. "Don't you know you can't steal from us?" He kicked me over so that I was lying face up. Then, he sat on me.

The air left my lungs in a rush. I gasped for breath, but my chest could not expand with so much weight on it. I felt my face growing red.

Duke clutched at my hand. I tried to fight against him. But he was much stronger. And with my head pounding in pain, it was easy for him to pry my fingers loose.

He held the coin up to one eye. He put it in his mouth and tried to bite. He jumped when it shocked his tongue.

"What the hell kind of coin is this?" he screamed at me. "What kind of coin *bites* you? Where'd you get it, boy? Who'd you steal it from?"

"I... didn't... steal it," I managed.

"Oh? Duke asked. "What? You shit it out, then?" He laughed. His friends laughed, too.

"It was given to me," I hissed. "It's mine! Give it back!"

Duke knocked my attempt away. "No." He tossed it to one of the brothers. "Go see how much old Atto will give you for it," he told him. "I reckon it should feed us a week."

"Duke, I think this is real gold," the boy said. A sudden grin split his face. "Can you imagine what we can get for it if it's *real gold*?"

"It ain't real gold, you idiot," Duke barked. "How many times your ma drop you on your head before she threw you out? Think! What would a kid like this be doing with a gold coin?"

"I'm just sayin', is all," the boy muttered.

"Didn't I tell you to run?" Duke roared. "What are you waiting for? GO!"

The boy turned and sprinted, taking my mark with him.

Rage erupted inside me. Rage at myself, for being so weak. Anger for being so stupid.

I fought to get out from under Duke to no effect.

That made him notice me again. "Look at him struggle, Butch!" His friend with the plank laughed.

Duke shifted his weight. It gave me just the space I needed. I pushed off the ground and popped out.

I would like to say that I sprang to my feet and ran after the boy with the coin. I would like to say that I caught him, fought him, and got my mark back.

But you have to remember how little food I'd had in the past week. You have to remember the state of my ankle, which hurt even more now than when I first sprained it. You have to remember the growing welt on the back of my head.

All I earned in lunging to my feet was a lurching stagger back to the ground.

Duke laughed mightily. "Look!" he cried. "Look, he can't even stand!" He grabbed the back of my shirt and hefted me up. Another rush of air left my lungs as he shoved me against one wall.

"Now look here," Duke said, trying to lower his voice to sound menacing. It still came out as a squeak. "I can tell you're new to the city. If you weren't, you woulda known better than to come into my territory. I'm going to teach you a few lessons. Lesson one—" he punched me in the stomach, causing me to double over, "*never* come on my turf. Lesson two—" he punched me again. I *oomphed*. "If any of us see you, we're going to beat you senseless. And lesson *three*—" he sent another blow that connected with my kidney, "you're *weak*, and I'm *strong*. Don't think you can change that."

He let go of my shoulders. I collapsed to the ground, clutching my middle. I heard him and his friend laugh as they walked away.

Something snapped inside me.

I was on my feet and running in seconds, flat. I didn't care that I made noise. Duke heard me coming at the last moment. By then, it was too late. I had a stone in my hand and was already in the air, flying at him.

My momentum knocked us both off balance. Duke hit the ground with a grunt. Clutching the stone, I went crazy. I bashed it against his head. I smashed it in his nose. It slipped out my fingers, and I clawed at his eyes, trying to gouge them out. His shock was so great that I even got a few decent swipes in.

My victory did not last long. His friend, who was still carrying that plank, took a swing at my back. The piece of wood snapped in two as the blow knocked me over. Duke rolled to his feet, roared, and barreled straight at me.

I had no chance. Duke was right: He *was* stronger than me. He was older, too, and much bigger. His fat shielded his vital organs, whereas my emaciated body did not provide such protection. His fist broke my nose. His elbow caught my jaw. His knee came up and struck me between the legs.

Even though I was young, that one sent me crumbling.

Still the beating continued. I huddled into myself as kick after kick landed on my body. His friend joined in, too, beating me with the remnant of that wooden plank.

As pain took over, and my consciousness slowly faded, the only thing I could conjure in my mind was the image of Alicia, choking on her own blood, dead because of me.

CHAPTER TEN

I thought I was dead.

I drifted in an abyss of emptiness. My body was so far away that I was not sure I would ever find it again.

The river of darkness swept me downstream like a leaf caught in the current. Every second that passed drew me farther and farther from the street where I lay.

I think one of my eyes flickered open when my ears picked up the faintest shuffling of feet. I saw two black-toed boots peeking out from under the curtain of a raggedy skirt.

Then I was being lifted. The sudden shift of position yanked me right back to the world of the living.

The pain that exploded along every inch of my body was unbearable. It was too much for my wakened mind to take. I passed out again.

***

I came to in a small, dark hut. The smell of arsenic floated heavy in the air.

A pair of hands, strong but deft, helped me sit up. My vision was blurry. A round, wooden mug was brought to my lips. I was too groggy to even notice the harsh, burning scent that the vapors gave off.

Suddenly, my nose was pinched, my head tipped back, and that drink poured down my throat.

How can I describe the concoction? Imagine you are an adventurer high on top of a cold mountain. You've run low on food and water. Topping a crest, you discover a magnificent sparkling blue pool.

You run to it. You kneel by its side. Warmth emanates from the water to heat your face.

The pool is fed by a hot spring active on the other side. You see steam rising from holes in the ground. You come up to one and wave a hand over it, testing the heat.

Then, in a moment, of severe indiscretion, you put your head above it and look down.

A geyser of hot, boiling water rushes out to greet you the moment you do.

That is what I felt when the liquid rolled down my throat. It burned like a trail of lava. It awoke all my slumbering senses.

I sputtered and choked, but the hands holding the cup to my face did not relent until I had swallowed every last drop.

"You're lucky I found you," a voice like rustling hay said. "Lucky the sight of your wretched body in the street pulled the strings of this woman's old and shrunken heart."

The hands let me go. I fell back, gasping for air. Heavy blankets covered my legs. I kicked them off. My body was producing heat to rival the greatest furnace.

Bit by bit, the sensation of burning lessened. Bit by bit, my rapid heartbeat slowed. I stared at the low, smoky ceiling of the hut and tried to piece together everything that had happened.

Duke and his friends beat me to an inch of my life. I have no doubt they thought they left me for dead. Somebody—this woman, presumably—found and cared for me.

Why? That was the prevailing question on my mind. *Why did she help me? Why didn't she let me die?*

I sat up, slowly, tense and ready for all the hurt I expected to feel. But I rose smoothly. Either the elixir worked its magic, or time had done its part.

"You've been with me eleven weeks," the woman offered, as if reading my mind. I turned toward her voice. "Eleven weeks old Magda has cared for you."

She was a shriveled old thing. For half a second, I was reminded of the gypsy woman who sold me to Three-Grin.

But Magda looked even older.

She stood no more than two inches above my height. Her back was crooked. Deep lines crowded her face. Her clothes were the clothes of a nun, though such dirty garments I had never seen in my life.

Her hands were hidden by long, gaping sleeves. They were stained an assortment of colors: here brown, there red, other places violet. She turned away and started moving around the room with the methodical efficiency of one very much at home, tending to the various instruments along the sides.

There were stoppered flasks and bubbling liquids. There were jars of drying leaves. There were clay pots and various tools:

scales and measuring sticks, chisels and augers, short bits of rope with equidistant knots tied in them. There were mortar and pestle sets of all sizes. There were piles of pretty rocks and fine powders. I saw a large, elaborate device with many small gears that fascinated me. I later learned it was for showing time.

Magda hummed a halting melody as she tended to her things. She pulled a single hair from her cap and dropped it in a pot of roiling water. She sanded her nails over the dried skin of a salamander.

"Do you know the common tongue?" she asked without looking my way.

I nodded even though I knew she could not see me. "Yes."

"Yes!" she echoed. "Then do speak up, boy. Tell me your name."

I debated lying, but instinct told me she would see through it. "Dagan."

"And where are you from, Dagan?" she asked. "Surely, not from here."

"No," I admitted.

She dipped a spoon into a tall clay jar and swirled it around. "So, Dagan-not-from-here, where *are* you from, hmm?" She turned toward me, and for a fleeting moment, her eyes reminded me of Karl's. "What business brings you to the *Great City of Hallengard*?" She managed to fill the title with all sorts of derisive scorn.

"I... I was told to come here," I said.

"Oh? Is that so? By whom?" It was easy to tell she did not believe me.

"A man," I answered.

"And did this man come to you in your dreams, maybe?" she laughed. "Did he speak to you while you slept?" She turned away and began tending her things again. "You know what I think, Dagan-not-from here? I think you're a runaway. That puts me in an awkward position. If somebody recognizes you on the street, I could get into a lot of trouble for sheltering you."

"I'm not a runaway," I protested.

"So you say, so you say," she nodded. "The question is: What can I do with you?" She went around the room as she spoke. "Or perhaps, the better question is: What can *you* do for me?"

I stalled.

"I spent eleven weeks nursing you to health. An effort like that should be rewarded, don't you think? So, Dagan-not-from-here, tell me: Have you any parents?"

"No."

"Do you know your letters?"

"No."

She tapped one foot. "Can you act? Sing? Steal?" Her eyes bore into me. "*Kill*?"

Could I kill? I remembered how easily the white-haired cart master went down. One arrow between the eyes was all it took. And I already had a list of targets enough to fit two hands: Three-

Grin, my three masked torturers. Duke, his friends. The gypsy woman.

"I can learn," I replied.

The woman clapped her hands together and hooted. "You can learn? Whoo-wee, boy! I'm starting to think that rescuing you was not such a mistake."

"Will you teach me?" I asked.

Magda frowned, taken aback by my question. "Me? No, no. I am old. Frail. These hands were made for healing—" she lifted them in front of her face and let the sleeves drop.

I gasped. Each hand had two fingers missing.

"—not killing," she concluded. "Although, at times, the difference between a potion and a poison is the skill of the administerer." She cackled. "And stealing?" She waggled her remaining fingers at me. "I learned at a young age that my hands were not deft enough for that. Four times I was caught. It took four fingers for me to learn that lesson."

Disappointment flared to life within me. Magda had brought me back from the abyss, but to what purpose?

She clicked her tongue. "Oh, don't look so glum, boy. Just because I can't teach you doesn't mean I don't know others who could."

My eyes shot up. I sat straighter.

Magda waved my enthusiasm away. "But, not yet. You've still got some healing to do before I let you back onto the city streets. How old are you?"

I cast my eyes downward. This was the second time I'd been asked the question I could not answer. "I don't know," I muttered.

"Head up, boy!" Magda snapped. "There's no shame in not knowing your own age, seeing as how nobody's ever told you. I don't take you to be dumb. So, that's the only other option, isn't it?"

She stepped up to me and peered into my eyes. I saw that hers were not black like Karl's, but instead a deep brown.

That comforted me.

"So, how about this?" Magda offered. "I tell you your age, and I reckon I'd be off by a year at most, if that. In return, you tell me how you wound up in Glorious Hallengard." She cackled again. "How does that sound? Fair?"

"Fair," I answered.

Magda nodded. "Thought so." She reached into a deep pocket and pulled out a flat, sanded piece of wood. It was about the length of a finger. She pressed it to my lips. "Open wide, now."

I did. She counted my teeth. Next, she told me to stand on the table and strip. I did. She flipped me over and tapped on each of my vertebrae, bringing her ear close to listen for the sound they made.

She counted my ribs, measured the girth of my neck, the length of my limbs, the distance from my bellybutton to my throat, and the circumference of my chest at the nipples.

When she was done, she told me to put my clothes back on. When I finished, she sat me down and looked deep in my eyes.

"By my reckoning," she told me, "you are just about to turn eight."

Eight. The number floated through the air and seemed to touch down onto me almost like a seal. It wrapped around my chest and infused me with strength I had lacked—or forgotten I had. It was a little piece of my identity that had been stolen from me.

Now, finally, I had it back.

Magna motioned to me. "Your turn."

I nodded, and told her my tale.

CHAPTER ELEVEN

"Hold on." Earl held up his hands. "You're sayin' a woman named *Magda* rescued you from the streets? What happened to the Arena?"

"Yeah," Patch agreed. "I thought you said before Three-Grin was raising you for it."

Dagan nodded impatiently. "He was."

"So what happened to all that training?" Earl asked. "To all your pain tolerance and such?"

"The year with Alicia softened me," Dagan answered. "My body had grown to withstand harsh conditions, but the moment the stimulus was taken away, the ability withered. When I reached Hallengard, I was just a regular boy."

"That ain't very good training if it be lost so easily," Earl muttered.

"Three-Grin did not mean for the training to last. He meant it to be thorough. He meant it so that his slave children would not die of shock the first time one of their limbs was severed in the Arena. He did it to give us an advantage of seconds. No more. In the Arena, the last to *die* wins. Two combatants enter. Neither leaves."

"You escaped the cart," Patch said. "The man who gave you the mark saved you! Doesn't that mean you weren't bound for the Arena anymore?"

Dagan shook his head. "The world is not so simple, Patch," he answered. "Fate had been watching me from the moment I was born. And fate decreed that my path would lead to the Arena."

***

A week later, Magda introduced me to Thraugh.

Thraugh was a boy two years younger than I was. But whereas I spent my childhood in a dungeon, Thraugh spent his on the streets. He was a veteran of the twisting alleys and rooftops of Hallengard.

Thraugh taught me a lot. He taught me to beg. He taught me to look after myself. He taught me to steal.

My first venture into the world of thievery was not an auspicious one. It earned me a whipping and a stained right thumb. That was the mark of a would-be thief in Hallengard. An unwritten code existed between the merchants and the urchins that every child would try his hand at thievery at one point or another

The merchants tolerated the first attempt, so long as you did not try again. The paint on my thumb was meant to be permanent, to signal to others that I had gotten my one free pass. The next time I was caught, I would lose a finger.

Magda laughed when she saw. She dressed the wounds on my back and dipped my thumb into a harsh solution that made it blister and burn. The skin peeled away a day later, but when it healed, there was no trace of the stain.

My second attempt was better. I feigned illness in the middle of a busy street. When the guard came to pick me up and carry me out of sight, I deftly cut the coin purse hanging from his waist.

I shared the money with Magda and Thraugh.

It did not take me long to surpass Thraugh in skill. I was motivated. I was fast. I had a mind ready to absorb anything thrown at it.

Magda stopped just short of offering me a home. Nevertheless, she had become someone I could rely on in times of need. While she did not give me food, she did show me all the places I could scavenge for scraps. She knew physiks, and thus could heal.

I relied on her for that. The first time I came to her with a fever and chills after biting into a fresh loaf of bread passed out by the

Church, she scolded me for being a fool and refused to treat me. She told me there were no free hand-outs in life. The ministers had spiked the bread with cyanide as a method of population control.

I spent all night shivering in a cold sweat. Sharp pains shot through my stomach. It was the longest night of my life. Not a single minute went by where I did not think I would die.

In the morning, Magda came outside and gave me a white, chalky drink that I gulped down in earnest. I spewed everything up moments after, including the poison that was killing me from within.

From that moment on, I ate only what I could buy with the little money I scraped together.

Most of my days were spent on street corners begging for iron pennies. I learned the places where people felt most generous, and the places where they were most stingy.

Most of my nights were spent cutting the purses of drunkards. I learned that though it was easier to steal from a drunk, nine times out of ten the amount of coin in their purse was hardly more than what I could earn in a day of begging.

As the months slowly passed, I grew more and more confident. I ventured past the familiar streets around Magda's hut, and discovered that all the places of Hallengard were mostly the same—at least, from the perspective of someone like me.

The first time I ventured into a gambling district, however, I thought I had found a new home.

No sooner had I sat down with my tin kettle placed in front of me (with some fake coins glued to the bottom to encourage donations), than a man burst out of a pub with two women on his arms. He was laughing and drinking from a mug held in one hand.

One of the women noticed me. She whispered a word to the man. He staggered over, reached into a purse, and dumped a handful of coins into my kettle.

He ruffled my hair as I stared, amazed, at my newfound fortune. "There ya go, you little hapless bastard," he laughed, slurring his words. "Enjoy some o' my winnings. " He turned away, put his arms around the women, and waltzed down the street.

I could not believe my eyes. I fingered the coins, doing a quick count. There were fifteen iron pennies, six copper marks, and one tiny, silver dime.

The dime was worth more than the rest put together. It was worth more than all the coins I'd ever collected put together.

Clutching my windfall, I got up and ran. I was going to go to Magda, to give her most of the coins as payment for everything she'd done. I could give her more than half, and still have enough to eat for a year.

I ducked through the sparse crowd, dodging legs and bodies, when suddenly a blow hit me right across the back.

I fell. The metal kettle flew out of my arms. The coins scattered.

Nobody paid me any mind—except for two large, heavyset street toughs.

"Look what we've got here," one of them said. "A little boy with a fortune. How'd you get all those coins, kid?"

"Say, these look like Delphic coins," the second said. "Now, how would a dirty little runt like you come across Delphic coins?"

"You're too young to gamble," the first mused. "So you must have stolen them, eh? Ahh, answer me!"

He picked me up and held me in the air, feet dangling. He smelled like smoke and rust and stone. "How did. You. Get those. *Coins*?"

"Someone gave them to me," I said, trying to squirm out of his grip. "Let go!"

"Someone gave them to you." He scoffed. "You spin a tall tale, kid. Why would anyone give so much money to a brat like you?"

"I think he stole it," his friend said over his shoulder. "We'll have to teach him what happens to thieves."

I remembered my blistering thumb. "No!" I screamed. "No, I didn't steal it!"

The man holding me tossed me down. I fell with a grunt. I could see my coins lying scattered around me. A space had cleared up on the street. The passersby were giving us a wide berth.

The two men towered over me like mountains. "The Delphic doesn't look kindly on stragglers, kid." A boot caught me in the side. "Get up! Collect your coins. We're going to hand them back to the casino."

I scrambled to pluck up as many as I could. My eyes searched wildly for the dime. I knew that if I could find it quickly, I had a chance of pocketing it without notice.

Luck was not on my side. The second of the toughs leaned down and picked a coin up. He flipped it in the air as he straightened.

I caught the slivery glimmer of my dime in the sun.

It represented half a year of food. It represented a warm place to sleep on cold nights. It represented a respite, however short, from life on the street.

The tough caught me looking. He scowled. "Did I tell you to stop? Get going!" He aimed another kick at my head, which I only narrowly avoided.

I collected the remaining coins under two pairs of watchful eyes. I clutched the little kettle to my chest protectively when I was done.

In the span of time it took me to retrieve the coins, I contemplated running a dozen times. And a dozen times, I reminded myself that I couldn't. I didn't know these streets. Even if I did, two grown men could easily outpace an eight-year-old boy.

I had no chance.

"Good," one of them said. He held out his hand. "Now, give me that kettle. Those coins belong to the Delphic, and that's where they'll go."

I held the kettle closer to my body. My eyes darted behind the men. If I went *that* way, however, I could find the path back.

Could I outrun them? I wasn't sure. But if I didn't try, regret would gnaw at me for weeks.

"No," I said, and sprang forward, ducking between the two men.

I passed under their legs, and for a brief, ephemeral moment, tasted freedom…

Then I was yanked off my feet and held up by the scruff of my neck.

The kettle was wrenched from my hands. I heard the clatter of coins inside as the street tough jerked it away. I heard warm nights and a full belly disappearing. I heard the promise of a slightly better life be whisked away.

"Smart-assed bastard tried to run," the one holding me said. "Can you believe that? I knew he was a thief."

The second cracked his knuckles. "We've got to teach the runt a lesson. He's gotta learn that we deal with thieves differently in the gambling district."

"Here." The man holding me tossed me to his friend as easily as if I was a coin purse. I collided with the second man's chest. He threw me over his back and turned away into an abandoned alley.

As he walked, I saw my kettle lying full and forgotten on the ground behind us.

CHAPTER TWELVE

He dumped me to the ground. My head bounced off the stone. My vision went wobbly for a few moments.

When I could see again, I saw the toughs staring down at me. They reminded me of two hungry cats circling a cornered hen.

The first one kicked at me. I braced myself against the blow before it landed. It caught me just beneath the ribs with enough force to send me flying against the wall.

"A thief and a smart-ass," he said. He kicked me again. "Let this be a lesson to you. Don't—" a kick, "—come—" another kick, "—to the—" one more, "—gambling district—again!"

He punctuated the last word with a heavy kick right into my stomach.

I curled up into myself, trying to protect my vital organs. The two toughs did not give me the privilege. One of them grabbed my shoulders and picked me up, then pinned me to the wall, exposing my body.

"You got that?" he snarled. His friend laughed as he landed a punch in the soft flesh of my gut. I doubled over in pain.

He released me and let me fall. I was treated to another flurry of kicks. My body started to go numb as I felt myself fading. Each kick seemed more distant than the last.

"…never… see… your face… again!"

The voices blended into an incoherent cacophony beyond the pain that consumed my world. A kick to the gut. A kick to the spleen. A kick to the back that sent me rolling. I tasted blood on my tongue and felt my entire body softening under the unrelenting blows.

I didn't know how long they beat me. I didn't even know how I was still alive. All I knew was that if I survived, two more people would be added to my revenge list.

***

Somehow, I found my way back to Magda in the dark. The trip was a blur. She cared for me, again, and when I was finally lucid enough to understand, scolded me for being so careless a second time.

I vowed that I would never be victim to a beating again.

After a few weeks, I was getting back to my regular self. I hadn't seen Thraugh since before my encounter with the toughs, and I felt a vague sort of concern for him.

It never grew into anything stronger. There was no room for sympathy in the streets.

Most nights, I slept behind a stack of crates sheltered in an alley corner. They were rotten and forgotten. Getting discovered there, or jumped in the night, was not a concern.

After I regained my strength, I went back to begging and thieving. I avoided other children, but always kept an eye out for Duke and his friends. They had something of mine, and though I didn't yet know how, I planned on getting it back.

And now, let me speak of the extenuating set of circumstances that brought me one step closer to that goal.

It was a day like any other. The sky was overcast with heavy clouds after a spring storm. Hunger had woken me early, and I ventured to one of the spots where begging was most fruitful.

The city of Hallengard was divided into two districts, as I've told you before. Magda's hut, clearly, was located in the south. My alleyway of crates was close by.

I have never been to north Hallengard.

The city is large enough that you can walk in a straight line for two days and still be within its walls. If fancy took you to make a turn, you could wander for three times that amount of time.

After losing my mark, nothing compelled me to seek out the grand structure in the heart of the city. Seeing it would only fill me with regret. Hallengard did not allow for self-pity.

I had barely spent an hour begging when a small, raggedy man approached me. His manner reminded me uncomfortably of Karl. He wore old, brown robes, stained with years of use. He had the same small, beady eyes.

Experience had taught me to be on my guard.

Without a word, he settled down a few feet away from me. I eyed him warily. He closed his eyes, took out a pipe, and started to smoke.

In those days, there were two types of leaves that people smoked. The first was called Angelherb. It was a small, brownish weed that sprouted in the cracks along buildings. When properly dried and crushed, it could be smoked for a brief, serene high that lasted anywhere from five to ten minutes.

After that, it made you violently sick.

I knew. One of the first things Thraugh showed me was how to roll Angelherb and smoke it without a pipe. The crash after the high was one of the most miserable experiences of my life.

The second leaf was called Devil's Bane. It was closely related to Angelherb, but much rarer—and thus, more prized. Devil's Bane gave you a clean, long-lasting high with no crash. When you smoked it, it was said that visions of otherworldly creatures came to your mind. You could hear them whispering in your ears.

Priests used Devil's Bane on a regular basis. They said it brought them closer to Xune.

That, of course, was a lie. But because of the susceptibility of the general public, it allowed the Church to control supply of Devil's Bane. They sold it only to their worshippers—and only enough for them to get the briefest high.

Devil's Bane was notoriously addictive. Whereas Angelherb had a kind of self-regulating mechanism, Devil's Bane had no such property. The Church leveraged that to extract money from the rich and increase its political power.

Angelherb and Devil's Bane were both distinguishable by the smell of their smoke. Angelherb gave off noxious, poisonous fumes. Devil's Bane had a sweet, slightly tart aroma.

From the smoke rising beside me, I could tell the man was smoking Devil's Bane.

That made me both curious and cautious. A beggar on the street could not afford Devil's Bane. Nobody in south Hallengard could. He must have stolen it—but eying him again, I could not imagine he had the deftness of hand or mind to pull off the caper. That meant he was somehow related to the Church.

Of course, there was also a third option. Alchemists in the city claimed to be able to refine Angelherb so that only the active ingredient remained. That was a load of horseshit. All they did was add scented chemicals to it that made the aroma somewhat reminiscent of Devil's Bane. It was not quite a perfect match, but, oftentimes, gullible junkies did not know any better...

Until the crash took them.

But, the man beside me smoked in silence for a good, long while. If it had been Angelherb, he would have exhibited the symptoms long ago.

The man stuck his pipe out at me. "You want a puff?" he asked. His eyes were still closed.

I had never tried Devil's Bane, of course. The offer intrigued me. I looked at the man, trying to determine if there was some way he could be masking the side effects of Angelherb.

When I decided 'No,' I took the pipe and cautiously inhaled.

The smoke was sweet and pure. It did not sting my throat as Angelherb would. In seconds, my world changed.

Colors became stronger. The day seemed less bleak. I felt strength gathering in my chest. It flowed out to encompass my limbs.

For a brief moment, I felt like I was floating. The constant worries at the back of my mind disappeared. I was freed from the shackles of poverty. The hunger in my stomach vanished. All I felt was a smooth, contented peace.

I brought the pipe back to my lips for a second draw, but had it jerked out of my fingers before I could.

"Nuh-uh-uh," the man giggled. "You want more, you have to do something for me."

A distant place of my mind went on high alert. That caution was immediately swept aside by the overwhelming desire for more Devil's Bane.

My face felt warm and flushed when I turned toward the man. In fact, my entire body felt warm. I could not recall the last time I had felt this good.

"What?" I asked.

"Oh, something simple, something simple," he muttered. He took out a folded envelope from an inside pocket. He held it in front of him and examined the seal. "Can you read?"

I shook my head. It seemed better to lie. In truth, Magda had been teaching me my letters, and I was a quick study.

But, I also guessed that if the man valued discretion, he'd be more likely to trust the letter to an illiterate.

"Good. Good! It's a simple task, my dearie." He giggled again. "I will point out a man to you. He passes this street every day. You will follow him. You must not be seen. Do you think you can do that?"

I nodded.

"Now, this man, he's a, hmm, a friend of mine. This letter—" he flourished it in my face, "—has to go to him, and him only. That is very important to me. But!" He jerked the letter back. "He cannot have it before nightfall. Do you understand? That is why I need you to follow him. Give this to him, at nightfall."

"If he's your friend," I said, "why can't you do it?"

The man gasped in shocked indignation.

"Oh, sweet boy," he said. "Sweet, silly boy. If I had time to do it myself, do you think I would ask this favor from one like you?" He lowered his voice. "This letter contains important words. *Written* words. A message. Do you understand? My friend *must* have it, but only after the sun has fallen from the sky. You want more of this, don't you?" He briefly crossed his eyes to look down at his pipe and rolled it around in his teeth. "If you do, return here tomorrow. *If* you deliver my letter—" He held it out to me again. "I will give you as much Devil's Bane as can fit in your pockets."

The man lifted a flap of his cloak and showed me the compartments sown inside. My eyes widened.

Each one was bursting with dry, pure clumps of Devil's Bane.

"Yes, sir," the man giggled. "Yes sir, you like what you see?" He lowered the cloak. "As much as you can carry. All yours, if you do this favor for me. That's not so hard now, is it? No. No, no, it's not. It's simple. Simple!"

"I can do it," I said, reaching for the letter. The man was not simply offering me Devil's Bane. He was offering me a fortune. If I could sell even a tenth of what he had… well, the lost dime paled in comparison to the money I could earn.

The man pulled the letter back just as my fingers brushed the sides.

"But!" he warned, "If you get caught, before nightfall, or somebody else sees the letter, you will lose *everything* you have. Do you understand?" His voice became harsh. "Do not disappoint me."

He broke off. "Oh, oh, look! Here he comes! Here he comes! Over there, in the tall hat."

I looked up and saw a man walking down the street with an arrogant strut. His upper lip was bare, but the rest of his jaw was covered by a thick, black beard. His mouth was twisted in what appeared to be a permanent expression of distaste.

The man beside me ducked and hid his face under one arm as his 'friend' passed. He ought not to have bothered. The man he wanted me to follow did not seem the kind to notice beggars.

My eyes trailed after him as he walked down the street. Here was a self-important buffoon if I've ever seen one. I looked back at my coconspirator, and discovered he had vanished. In his spot lay the sealed envelope.

I grabbed it and stuffed it into one of my inseam pockets. I'd learned the importance of having an abundance of little hiding places on your person my first week on the Hallengard streets. Every chance I got, I brought a little string to Magda and asked her to sew another one for me.

I looked up. The man I was supposed to follow was already gone. I wasn't worried. His face was distinctive enough that I could pick him out of a crowd at a glance.

I turned and scaled the wall. Right foot, small crack. Left foot, protruding brick. I was on the rooftop in a flash, and I ran the way I had seen the man walking.

Sure enough, I found him strutting through the crowd on the other side. A baker hawking meat pies nearly shoved one in his face. He grimaced and stepped around the fat man.

As I followed him, my mind kept turning back to all the Devil's Bane I was offered. It was a well-known fact that anyone could hire a street urchin to run some insignificant errand on his behalf. A ha'penny was all it took.

Why would the man offer me what amounted to more than a thousand times the price?

I ran, jumped, and climbed on autopilot. All the while, my mind struggled with the question. One answer was that this task was extremely dangerous—though how or why, I did not know. Another was that the Devil's Bane was fake, and the man who offered it was trying to swindle me by hooking me with a pipe full of the real thing.

I valued caution over luck and miserliness over generosity. The more I thought on it, the less the offer made sense.

I settled down atop the edge of a roof, my feet hanging in the air, as the bearded man entered a brothel. I expected I would be waiting a while.

I took out the envelope and looked it over.

It was made of thick, brown paper. I held it up to the sun, even though I already knew I could not see through it. The flap was sealed with a blob of wax. There was no sigil imprinted in it, as would be customary in those times.

I fished out a small butter knife I had found discarded a week prior. I pushed it underneath the flap and eased it open.

I cringed when a piece of the envelope tore with the wax. There was no way of salvaging it other than finding a new envelope. And paper was much too expensive for me.

But, figuring what's done is done, I shrugged and took the letter out.

I expected to find a written message inside. What I saw instead shocked me so much that I nearly let the wind sweep the sheet out of my hands.

There was a single 'X' in the middle of the page writ in blood.

I'd been in the city long enough to hear of such things. The secretive Black Brotherhood—also known as the assassin's guild—sent out letters like these to targets who've had a hit placed on their heads. It was a warning, but also an offer: *Beat the price we've been given, and we will not kill you.*

Those who failed to do so died within twenty-four hours.

My mind reeled with the implications. For one, it meant that the Black Brotherhood was real. The most anyone could confirm of their existence came in whispers spoken in dark, hidden places. Revealing the Black Brotherhood's secrets was a crime punishable by death.

Of course, everything about them might also be a hoax. Unscrupulous con men could be sending letters like this to extract money from frightened nobles. The rumors about the letters could have been planted by them long ago. A rumor that is repeated often enough frequently takes on the appearance of truth.

But I was not willing to rest on that assumption.

The more unsettling thought was that *I* was in possession of the letter. *I* had seen the red cross.

Had somebody put a bounty on *my* life?

Was the story about delivering the letter just some elaborate ploy to get it into my hands? Did the man who gave it to me simply rely on my curiosity for me to open it?

I heard a fluttering of wings behind me and jumped, spooked out of my mind. A raven cocked its head at me.

Caw! Caw!

"Stupid bird," I muttered. I picked up a rock and expertly threw it a foot above its head.

The sudden movement startled the raven. It opened its wings and flew up in the air.

My rock connected with its skull.

It dropped back down, dead. Just to make sure, I walked over and wrung its neck, then hid it inside a nearby chimney. There was good meat on those bones, and I intended to bring it back to Magda to make a soup.

If the Black Brotherhood was not coming to get me.

I went back to the ledge and scanned the crowd. No sign of the man I was following. Good. If he was still inside, that gave me time to think.

I crouched down and rocked on my heels, ready to spring away at a moment's notice. If I saw so much as a shadow behind me...

Suddenly, the ludicrousness of my fear occurred to me. It made me laugh. I could not run from professional assassins. But, more importantly, if someone *really* wanted to kill me, they wouldn't waste time or money going through the Black Brotherhood. I had nothing to my name. The letter with the cross meant nothing to me. There was no way I could afford to pay.

I doubted an organization as revered as the Black Brotherhood would even entertain the notion of wasting their talents on a kid. If someone wanted me dead, it wasn't hard to accomplish. Nobody in south Hallengard would bat an eye if they found the body of a boy stuffed in the back of some alley.

This presented me with yet another choice.

If I were to assume that the Black Brotherhood was real, and that the man I was following really was a target, it meant that he had money.

I was supposed to give the letter to him at nightfall. If I delivered it earlier, as a warning, would he consider rewarding me for it?

I doubted I would see the man with the Devil's Bane again. Why would he pay *me*, a nobody, after I had done what he wanted? I was a fool for accepting. Yet I could still make my choice about how I wanted to proceed.

I mulled over my options while seated on my haunches. I could throw the letter away and simply forget about it. I would avoid the street where the giggly man found me. I could pretend it never happened.

That seemed like the coward's way out.

I could follow directions and deliver the letter at nightfall. I did not know the significance of waiting that long. Presumably, it would give the man less time to decide if he would pay off the hit.

Or, I could take my chances and find him now. I could give him the letter and hope he would reward me somehow for alerting him early.

That last option seemed like the best bet. Even if I didn't get anything out of it, I would be done with this troublesome business for good. There were still hours left in the day. I could go back to begging and hope to salvage some more coin.

I nodded to myself, decision made. I put the letter, unsealed, back in my pocket. Then, I climbed down and started for the brothel.

In my mind, it would be as easy as walking through the front doors, finding the man, handing him the letter, and accepting my reward.

Of course, real life never works that way.

I was yanked off my feet just as I was about to reach the door. A city guard I had foolishly overlooked scowled at me.

"Where d'ya think yer goin', you little runt? This is a fine establishment for payin' customers. If you think you'll find yer ma in there, you've got 'nother thing coming."

He carried me to an alleyway and dumped me to the ground. "Go on, git outta here. I'm paid t'keep the peace, and you be disturbin' it." He gave me a shove between the shoulder blades. "Run along, now. Go t' wherever your came from, and don't let me see yer ugly mug around here again. Got it?"

He turned and went to his post.

All in all, that was probably the nicest I've ever been treated by a guard.

I scurried down the alley in the opposite direction and looked for a wall I could scale. I found one quickly. In seconds, I was back on the rooftops, searching for an alternate way in.

The brothel was a large, low building that occupied an entire block. The street in front of it was busy and crowded. Two alleys ran along the sides, each coming to a dead end. The area behind it housed a walled garden.

That garden was my way in.

I didn't know how much longer I had before the man I was told to follow left. And while I knew that the place he entered was *called* a brothel, I had no idea of what actually went on inside. I assumed it was an upscale kind of tavern that catered to both ladies and gentlemen.

In the end, I decided that if I missed him while trying to go round back, it would not be the end of the world.

I dropped down before the garden wall and walked across to it. It was tall and made of bricks. I brushed my fingers over it. I could get a bit of a handhold, but not enough to climb all the way up.

I looked around, and discovered an old tree.

It grew close to one corner. The unpruned branches reached the other side.

I ran up to it and jumped. My hands caught the lowest branch, and I pulled myself up. The branches bent but did not snap under my weight. For the first time in my life, I was actually glad I was not bigger.

The garden was full of bushes double the height of a man. They outlined a path that looked a bit of a maze.

I heard laughter from around a corner in front of me, and quickly darted under one of the shrubs.

I watched, careful to temper my breathing, as a beautiful young woman appeared along the path. She was pulling a man after her while giggling and trying to hold in her delighted laughter.

When I saw who he was, my eyes nearly fell out of my head. I could not believe my luck. He was the one I was told to follow.

The bearded man stopped almost directly in front of me and pulled the woman back into his arms. She melted into his embrace and latched her mouth onto his.

As I watched, the tiniest spark of jealousy lit within me. The woman was beautiful. The man was decidedly not.

I chose to interrupt them before they got too carried away.

I emerged from my spot by the ground, shaking the bush. The sound alerted the woman. She broke away and screamed when her eyes fell on me.

I would have reacted the same way if I were in her shoes. The sight of me—dirty, raggedy, small—must have been traumatic to someone used to the privacy of the garden and the company of high-class men.

The man looked my way. He did not seem surprised.

"You are the boy who's been following me," he observed. His voice was rich and deep.

I misplaced my step and stumbled forward. I could not hide the shock on my face. He knew? *How*?

"Miranda, run back inside, will you?" the man said. His eyes remained fixed on me. "Wait for me in your room. If I do not return within the hour, continue with your day. It means I am done with you." He pressed a coin into her hand. I caught the glitter of gold.

She picked up her skirts and made as if to run, but the man caught her arm. He put one more coin in her hand.

"A token," he said, "of your assured silence." He gestured to me.

She swallowed, bobbed her head up and down, and ran off.

I was left alone with him. His gaze paralyzed me. His eyes were dark, but nothing at all like Karl's had been. These eyes did not miss a thing.

He squatted down and looked at me.

"So, boy, I take it you have something for me?" He held out one hand, palm-up. "I'll be taking it now, thank you."

I took a tiny step back. Something about the man screamed,
Danger!

It was not the sort of danger that Three-Grin evoked. That type of
danger was like a rabid dog. You knew what the threat was as
soon as you saw it.

This danger was more subtle. It was the danger you feel when
you stare into the eyes of a resting lion. It is the unspoken threat
of harm from one who knows he is more powerful than you. It is
the danger that comes with the wind on an icy night.

The man cocked his head to one side. "No? Have you changed
your mind?" He stood up and stretched his arms overhead.
"That's a shame. Curiosity is a powerful thing."

I looked at the towering wall to one side. I glanced up, and saw
the branch I used to drop in.

The man noticed the movement of my eyes. "Ahh," he said.
"Thinking of an escape, are you?"

He gestured to the wall. "You are boxed in. The only way out is through the front door, though the appearance of someone like you inside the building would cause a magnificent stir. Let's see…" he tapped his lips, "…trespassing on private property. Disruption of the peace. Hmm." He crossed his arms. "If you were slightly older, perhaps I would say you would get away with a whipping. Maybe the guards would chalk your appearance up to idle curiosity. But you must be what? Six? Seven?"

"Eight," I said defiantly.

"Eight." The man's face shadowed. "A dangerous age. Not yet old enough to be a man, but too old to be a child. Have you heard of the galleys, boy?"

I nodded.

"The proprietor here isn't a fan of younglings. But he is friends with the city guard. Now, a life chained to an oar, for your simple crime, seems a little harsh to me. But, that is exactly what I think you'll face if you take your chances and run.

"You see, from the perspective of the owner, you are a pest. He likes to keep a clean establishment. Any vermin he finds," the man flicked off a ladybug that had landed on his shoulder, "needs to be eliminated immediately, lest the infestation spread. Do you understand?"

I swallowed and nodded.

The man shrugged. "He'll pull some strings, fill a few purses. Before you know it, you'll be on the deck of some bloody ship, oaring away for the remainder of your sad, miserable life. Do you understand what I'm saying?"

I glanced past the man, but we were still alone. "Yes."

"Now, your other option—" he knelt down again, "—is to befriend me. Nobody will protest if I walk in there with you. Nobody will dare raise a hand. The question is—" he exhaled meaningfully, "—which path of two evils will you take?"

I thought about it for a long time. Then, instead of answering, I asked a question.

"How did you know I followed you?"

The man laughed. "You cut right to the point, don't you? I have eyes and ears, boy. I learned to use them before I was your age."

A more unsatisfying answer I could not imagine. I was *sure* I had followed him unseen. He did not glance up at the rooftops once!

"Can you teach me?" I asked.

That surprised the man. His brows knotted up. "And what would I get in return?"

"This," I said. I took out the letter. "As a warning."

He took the envelope from my hand. He did not question the open seal. He unfolded the letter, looked at it for a second, then closed his eyes in thought.

Eventually, he exhaled. "This is why you were trailing me?"

I nodded.

"When were you given this?"

"This morning."

"And when were you supposed to hand it to me?"

"At nightfall."

"Then you are either the greatest fool in the world or the paragon of bravery." He barked an incredulous laugh. "Do you know what 'paragon' means, boy?"

I shook my head.

He waved it away. "It doesn't matter. Nightfall, you say?" He stood up and started walking down the path. "Come on," he called out over his shoulder.

I ran to catch up. "Where are you going?"

"To show that I'm not afraid."

I had to hurry to keep up with his long strides. "What?"

"The Black Brotherhood thinks they can frighten me. I will show them otherwise."

"You mean, they're *actually* real?"

The man scoffed. "Yes. But much less fearsome than the stories." We reached the building. He opened the door and I ducked inside after him. I saw lush pillows and richly-decorated chaises. There were women, some of whom were only half-clothed. I gaped until the man grabbed my shoulder and pulled me away.

"First rule," he said, "never stare. It concedes your power. Also makes you look like a boy still wet around the ears." He retrieved his coat from a hook, threw it over his shoulders, and walked outside.

The guard who was standing post did a double take when he saw me. He started to rise, but one placating hand gesture from the man I was following made him sit back down.

The bearded man strode to the middle of the street. He shielded his eyes as he looked up at the sky and scanned the rooftops. "If you had not strayed from your instructions," he asked me, "where would you be right now?"

"You mean, if I was still trying to follow you?"

"Yes."

I pointed to the roof of one building. "Right there."

The man looked at the spot and frowned. "Reckless," he murmured. He shook his head and looked down at me. "You have a lot to learn, boy."

He fished the envelope out of his pocket and took out a match. He bent down and struck it against the cobblestone. It flared to life.

He held the flame to one corner of the letter until it caught. He straightened, and held the burning paper high above his head.

Several people cast him strange looks as they passed.

"What are you doing?" I asked.

"Rejecting their offer. If the Black Brotherhood thinks they can extort money from me…" he laughed. "Then they don't know me very well."

The man did one slow turn, holding the burning envelope overhead, then released it and let it fall to the ground. As soon as it hit the street, the whole thing burst into a ball of flame. It didn't take long for it to be incinerated.

"How'd you do that?" I asked.

"Not me," he shook his head. "*Them*. They infused the blood with a combustible chemical." He pointed up to the trail of smoke rising from the ground. "It gives off a white plume like that when it burns."

"So they can see that you burned it? What if they're not watching?"

"You think you are the only one following me?" The man did not wait for me to answer before striding down the street. Once more, I had to run to catch up.

"The Black Brotherhood is not a band of assassins, but thieves," the man explained as I dodged walkers to stay by his side. "They know how to frighten people. They also know how the stalk the shadows unseen. At least," he offered, "to those who don't know what to watch for."

He turned at an intersection and hailed a coach. One with a team of four horses stopped beside us. He climbed on and held out his hand to me. "Are you coming?"

I looked both ways, suddenly wary of having a tail, and nodded. The man clasped my arm and pulled me up.

"To Lamore Tavern," he told the driver.

The man swung the reins, clicked his tongue, and we were off.

CHAPTER THIRTEEN

The ride took us over an hour, though time passed in a flash. From the back of a coach like this one, Hallengard seemed foreign to me.

For once, I wasn't running out of the way to avoid being trampled. I looked with wide eyes at every building we passed.

We took the main road that ran north. I tensed without realizing it when we passed the street where Duke and his friends beat me. The man noticed and touched my shoulder.

I jumped in surprise. Our eyes met. He didn't say a word, but his irises carried such a steady calm that they comforted me.

I kept a watch out for Duke, but of course, didn't see him. The rattling wheels of a coach always send the urchins running. The drivers are known for not slowing down for those who get in the way.

I was so entranced by the surrounding buildings that I did not notice when the road curved and opened to a wide, magnificent street.

I looked up and sucked in an awed breath. Far in the distance, a great cathedral stood. The road split around it the way a river does around an enormous boulder.

The cathedral had a single tower. I had seen the peak from south Hallengard before, but had never connected it to this structure. It was obviously the building the man who gave me the mark had spoken of.

"The great library of Rel'ghar," the man beside me said when he noticed me staring. "Built in tribute to the fallen city. The architects tried to mimic the splendor of that hallowed place, but no hands of men could build anything to compare."

"Who owns it?" I asked.

The man laughed. "Nobody owns it. The first monarch of Hallengard decreed that a space be reserved in the heart of a city as a monument to Rel'ghar. It is the only land he gave away. It is a public place of learning, open to all. Great stacks of books line what are called the crypts underground. They are tended by the Rel'aille. Any member of the public can go inside and request a book on any subject they desire. The Rel'aille go down to the crypts and retrieve it. It is said that the entirety of human knowledge is contained in the pages of those tomes."

"Is it true?" I asked, my eyes wide.

The man chuckled. "To an extent, I suppose. None know for sure—save the Rel'aille. They are the only ones to have seen the stacks."

He lowered his voice. "I have heard it said that a man can spend his entire life reading and not make it through a hundredth of the books contained in there."

"That's impossible," I huffed. The most books I had ever seen were in Magda's hut, and I could count all of them with the fingers of one hand.

"Maybe so," the man offered. "But if no one believes in the impossible, what would any of us dream of?"

That thought made me sit back, stumped.

We rode the rest of the way in silence. I wondered how someone became a Rel'aille. I wondered if that was what my mark would have granted me.

Most of all, I was fascinated by the idea of all those books. I had a naturally inquisitive mind. I knew of the way Magda treasured her books. A single book could contain knowledge gathered over a lifetime. If I could properly read, I could obtain that knowledge myself. I could learn what others know. I could learn from the mistakes they had made and experiences they had had.

Above all, I could earn myself an advantage very few took the time to exploit.

What did I want most in my life? The answer came easily: Revenge. I wanted revenge against Three-Grin for the way he killed Alicia. I wanted revenge against all those who had ever wronged me. Perhaps it was not the healthiest state of mind for a boy my age. But, that desire molded me into the man I am today.

Not that my life is something to aspire toward. Quite the opposite. But in certain times, it does make for an entertaining tale.

The coach jolted to a stop in front of a side street. "Lamore's that way." Our driver jerked a thumb across his shoulders. "But this is the farthest my horses will bring you."

"Fine," the man beside me said. He paid the driver and stepped off. I went with him.

"Do you have a name?" he asked me as we started down the street.

"Dagan," I replied, looking around. "Where are we going?"

"Where all men go when they know the hour of their death is nigh." The man grinned at me. "We are going to drink!"

Chapter Fourteen

Lamore's Tavern was a shabby, dark place. When we entered, a wiry man behind the counter shot me an appraising look. He did not object, however, as I sat down.

The man whose name I still didn't know pressed four silver dimes on the table. I stared at the coins. The bartender took them without a word, bent down, and produced two large pitchers of drink, foaming at the top.

"One's for you," the man said, pushing it toward me.

My hand gripped the handle. My mind grappled with the fact that I held, in one hand, a drink that was worth *two* silver dimes.

The man brought his up to his lips and took a swallow. He exhaled in pleasure.

"Go on," he told me. "It's quite good."

I nodded and sat higher on the stool. I pulled the mug closer. The bubbling liquid seemed to hiss at me. I bent over it and sucked in a small sip.

I blanched and spat it back out. The taste was revolting.

The man, who was watching for my reaction with a close eye, clapped my back and laughed. "Too strong for you?"

I nodded while gagging.

He dragged my drink back to him. "At least now you know you're not missing out."

I watched, fascinated, as he brought the ale to his face and chugged it whole. When he was done, he set it back onto the counter with a *thud*. He wiped away the foam that covered his bare upper lip.

"Gods, that's good," he said.

"Gods?" I asked. "I thought there was only one. Xune?"

"Xune is the most widely known, and the most revered," the man said, "but he is far from the only god."

I blinked. "There are others?"

The man moved his hand in a vague, circular motion. "Have you ever glanced up at the stars at night, Dagan? Do you know what all those tiny lights are?"

I shook my head. "I never thought about it."

"The legend goes," the man said, "that once, the earth was the very home of the gods. They lived in peace and harmony, except for one:

"Xune."

Xune was not the strongest, nor the fastest. He could not move mountains like his brother, Oridon, nor split the seas like his sister, Fellaira. He could not fly with the birds like Aerogan, nor speak to the trees like Possmar.

But he had one trait the others lacked: a sharp cunning. Xune was the trickster. He delighted in playing pranks on his brothers and sisters.

He would conjure illusions of mountains and laugh when Oridon tried to restore them to their rightful place. He would whisper in the ears of Possmar and pretend to be nature itself.

At first, the other gods tolerated Xune's jokes. He was the youngest, they said, and he had inherited the least. Let him have his fun.

But over the centuries, Xune's tricks became more malicious. He would make the seas boil and kill all the creatures who called them home. He would call upon thunderstorms to strike down anything with wings.

He was ruining the peace the other gods had created. He did not understand how his brothers and sisters enjoyed living such sterile lives. He craved disorder and chaos because that brought excitement.

One day, while strolling through the woods, he heard two of his brothers approaching. Quickly, he camouflaged himself in the trees. Their hushed voices told Xune they did not want to be heard, and thus, he was eager to eavesdrop.

They spoke of a secret meeting taking place that night. All the gods were invited—save for him.

Xune grew furious. Was he not, too, one of their kin? Did he not, also, deserve his rightful place among them?

He stalked his brothers to find out more. The meeting would take place at the peak of Allhur, the greatest mountain in the world. It was said that the peak reached so high that from the top, you could stretch out and touch the moon.

Xune had never been to Allhur. It was Oridon's home. Even Xune respected such boundaries. But he would not sit back and watch while his brothers and sisters gathered without him.

He ran to the mountain before everybody else. He snuck past the watchful eye of Oridon and crouched low among the jagged rocks. He waited.

When night came, and the first gods began to arrive, Xune held his breath. He did not want to be discovered until everyone was there.

He waited until all the gods had gathered at the peak of the mountain. Just as he was about to rise from the shadows and make himself known, he heard his name spoken.

He froze, and listened.

Oridon was the orator. He spoke of how Xune's tricks were becoming tiresome. He spoke of how Xune's desires clashed with those of the other god's. He spoke of how Xune did not belong.

Suddenly, Xune understood why he had not been invited. It was a trial against him. It was where judgment would be made.

Xune grew outraged. He leapt from his hiding spot and startled the gods.

"Oridon," he screamed, "your treachery is unbound!" He spun on the others. "Possmar, I banish you. Leave this earth and never come back.

"Aerogan, I banish you. Leave this earth and never come back.

"Fellaira, I banish you. Leave this earth and never come back."

And so he named all the gods in sequence, uttering the forbidden words that would strip them of their power. They were too shocked to act, or perhaps Xune was too quick.

He named all of them except Oridon, for he knew his power was weakest in his brother's domain. If he tried the same trick on Oridon, the spell he cast on the others would break.

Oridon could restore them, too, so Xune knew he had to speak fast.

"Brother, you have forsaken me," Xune said. "And inspired the hot pillar of my rage. But perhaps I was too rash. Claim me as your own again, and all of this can be undone."

Oridon remained wary of Xune. He had fallen victim to too many of his brother's tricks.

"I can undo what has been done," he said. "So tell me, brother, what need have I of you?"

"You have the same need of me as you have of all your kin," Xune answered. "I am not less."

Oridon did not move. "Repent all you have done, and swear you will trouble us no more with your trickery. Only then will I welcome you back as my blood."

Xune fell to his knees and swore. He confessed everything, from setting the plagues that ruined crops to causing tremors that tore the earth open. Oridon was so touched by the honesty that he clasped Xune by the shoulder and begged him to rise.

But Xune had one more trick up his sleeve. As soon as his brother touched him, a link was formed between the two gods. The link combined their individual power. Xune stretched out his hand and called for Oridon's mighty hammer. It flew through the air, into his palm.

Oridon's shock was immense. Never before have any of the gods wielded weapons of one of their kin. He tried to pull back to sever the connection, but found Xune's fingers digging around his wrist.

"Oridon," Xune spoke, "I banish you from this earth. Leave, and never come back."

Oridon froze. Xune swung the hammer at his head, and shattered it into a thousand tiny fragments.

Then he rose, and laughed. The other gods remained frozen in their bodies, unable to move anything except their eyes. They stared at Xune and could not believe his madness.

But Xune did not care. He came up to the locked body of every god and swung Oridon's hammer. One by one, he shattered all of them, until only his sister Fellaira was left.

She could not speak, but her eyes begged him to stop.

Xune raised the mighty hammer. He started the downward sweep that would destroy her.

But at the last moment, he caught a reflection of his rage glimmering in her pupils.

He shifted the blow. The hammer swept by her face and landed amongst the rocks. Xune embraced his sister and spoke. "Fellaira, I release you. Save me from what I have done. Fellaira, I free you. Come back to this earth. Fellaira, I submit to you. Punish me as you see fit."

Fellaira was the wisest of the gods. When she was released from Xune's spell, she did not address him. She gathered the fragments of her siblings and flung them into the sky.

Then she turned to Xune. "Your punishment is to remain alone on the earth you so craved. Your punishment is to walk the barren fields with no hope of seeing life again. Your punishment is to be left forever on this frozen rock, while we, your siblings, watch from the heavens and forever judge you for your sins."

With that, she leapt into the sky, and disappeared beyond the dark face of the moon.

Xune stood and surveyed the land. The earth was his. He could finally do as he pleased.

He assumed the thought would bring him satisfaction, but it only carried sadness. With no witnesses to his pranks, why would he even bother?

Melancholy touched him as he walked down the mountain. But when he turned back to look upon Allhur one last time, he saw a sparkle of dust that Fellaira had forgotten.

He rushed to it, and saw that Fellaira had not forgotten it at all, but rather left it for him. He picked it up. It contained a tiny piece of every god who now watched him from above.

Xune was devious and cunning, so he formed a plot that would restore life to the earth. Out of the dust, he formed tiny standing figurines representing each of the twelve gods. He brought two— one male, and one female—to each corner of the earth, and whispered the words that would breathe new life into them.

Xune had created the world's first humans.

His creations rose, but not very high. They were like the gods in appearance, but otherwise smaller, frailer, and weaker. They did not possess any of the powers Xune's brothers and sisters once had.

He retreated to Allhur, where he remains to this day. And every night, it's said that the sparkling stars in the sky are the remnants of his brothers and sisters, watching, judging, and looking down upon us.

CHAPTER FIFTEEN

"That's what the stars are?" I asked. "Pieces of other gods?"

"So the legend goes," the man replied. He had finished his drinks and just put more coins on the bar for the next round.

The bartender refilled both pitchers. The man picked them up, stood, and motioned to a far, empty corner. I followed him there. We settled down at a table not unlike this one.

He leaned back and kicked both feet up. He drank from one pitcher. I watched him. He drank from the other.

The anticipation was killing me. Finally, I burst out, "Aren't you going to do something?"

The man quirked an eyebrow at me. "I am." He motioned to the drinks. "I've told a story, and now I am getting uproariously drunk."

"Not that!" I hissed. "I mean about the—" I lowered my voice, "—Black Brotherhood."

The man raised his shoulders in an elaborate shrug. "They'll find me in due time."

"So you're just going to *wait* for them?" The incredulity was clear in my voice.

He motioned around the tavern. "Better wait in a place of my choosing than one of theirs, don't you think?" He took another swig.

"But they're coming to *kill* you," I protested. "Aren't you worried? Aren't you going to *prepare*?"

"Prepare to die?" he humored me. "I don't think any man alive wants to prepare for that."

"Then what are you *doing*?"

He leaned forward. "You want the truth? I'm passing time. Not only do I have to watch for my own skin tonight, but I have to babysit you, too."

I crossed my arms and stuck my chin out. "I'm not a baby."

"You couldn't swallow your drink."

"I didn't like it."

He cocked his ear toward me. "What was that? All I could hear was *wah, wah*."

I was growing *incredibly* frustrated. "Why are we here?" I asked.

"Come, Dagan. I've told you the answer to that three times."

"I mean, why are we *really* here?" I corrected. "You're not just going to wait for the Black Brotherhood to come and kill you!"

"Why not?"

I stood up. "I'm leaving. I—"

The man caught my arm. I had no idea how he moved so fast. One minute he was leaning back in his seat, the next, he was hovering over me like an angry deity.

"*Not* a good idea, kid," he said. His eyes darted to the barkeeper. "You see him? He knows you came in with me. He looks like the type ready to divulge information, especially given a little…" He twisted my arm enough for pain to shoot up the limb, "…forceful persuasion."

He let me go. "So sit down. You know our coach was followed, yes?"

"It was?"

"Of course it was," he snapped. "Stupid boy. Why did you think I hired the largest one and took the main road? If I had intentions to disappear, that is not how I would have done it."

"So why didn't you?" I asked. Then it dawned on me. "Wait. You're looking for a fight!"

"And finally, Dagan proves he's not an idiot," the man announced. "Congratulations. Have a drink. On me." He pushed his across the table.

He was mocking me. But suddenly, I had a new respect for him. He knew the Black Brotherhood was coming, and did not cower and hide.

He'd been right: We took the most ostentatious means of transportation possible to Lamore's Tavern. He was making it easy for the assassins to find him.

The question was: *Why*?

"Who are you?" I whispered.

The man laughed. "Finally, you're asking the right questions. But your curiosity is misguided. *Who* I am does not matter. A man can change names the way a serpent sheds skins. What I can do, however..." he trailed off and peered into his drink, "...*that* is the important question."

"So, what *can* you do?"

A knowing smile played on his lips. "Would you like a demonstration?"

I had a feeling we were playing a dangerous game. Despite that, I nodded.

"Stand up, then, Dagan. Walk over to that wall."

I did. I walked to the wall closest to us and turned around. "Now what?"

"Now... catch this apple!"

He produced an apple from the inside of his coat and tossed it to me. It arced high through the air. I cupped my hands out to catch it...

And never got the chance. A knife whizzed through the air and split the apple in two. The blade sunk into the plank behind me, a hair's breadth above my head.

I could feel the vibration of the quivering metal against my skull.

The two pieces of the apple fell to the floor. I looked at them in wonder, and then looked back at the man. I didn't dare move my head for fear of being cut.

He had his face hidden behind the pitcher he was busy downing.

I ducked down and ran to him. "That was amazing! How did you do that? That was—"

"Nuh-uh," he stopped me. He pointed to the wall. "My knife, please."

I hurried back to it and gripped the hilt. I turned back without thinking, pulled—

And ended up flat on my ass when the blade didn't give.

The man laughed. "Come on, Dagan! I know you've got more strength in those arms than that!"

I scowled as my face turned bright red. I stood up, wrapped both hands around the hilt, and pulled again.

It didn't budge.

I gritted my teeth and tried once more. I put one foot against the wall as leverage and used it to push. My whole body strained as I tried desperately to yank the knife out of the wood.

It was no use. The blade was stuck as solidly as if it had been forced in with a hammer.

"Trouble?" the man asked over my back, surprising me. I looked up to find him standing beside me. "My turn."

He put his thumb and forefinger on the blade and gave the most delicate of tugs.

It came out as if the wood were merely butter.

My jaw hung open as I trailed the man back to the table. His coat swished around him as he sat down.

He noticed me staring. "Impressed?"

I spoke so quickly I stumbled over the words. "How did you do that? How did you get the knife in your hand so quickly? How did you throw it so fast? How did you know I wouldn't move?"

"I didn't," he replied solemnly. "You can never know something with absolute certainty. But I've been watching you since we met. You did not seem like the kind to jump."

I remembered the raven I'd killed. "But if I had—"

"Then I'd be explaining to the barkeeper right now why there's a dead kid lying on the floor of his tavern." The man laughed. "But I thought you had more guts than that. I'm pleased to see that I was right."

I didn't know whether to be affronted or satisfied with the compliment. I decided on the middle ground, going for indifferent.

"How'd you get it out of the wood?" I asked. "Are you really that much stronger than me, or was that—"

"—a trick?" He finished. "What do you think, Dagan?"

"I don't think you're that much stronger than me."

The man grinned. "Self-assured as always. I like that. You're right. I'm the only one who could have removed the blade from the wall." He laughed again. "Unless they took to the beam with an axe."

"How?" I asked. "Was it... *magic*?"

"After a fashion, I suppose."

I looked at him again in awe. The man knew magic. *Real* magic.

"If you're thinking of asking me to teach you, the answer is *no*," he said.

My face fell.

"At least, not yet," he corrected gently. "There are many levels of training you have to go through before you can be trusted with learning the elemental seals."

"The elemental seals?" I asked. "What are those?"

"A method of binding earth, air, fire, and water. All the material you see around you consists of those four building blocks. From that apple—" He gestured behind me. "—to this wood." He rapped his knuckles against the table.

"And you know all that?" I asked, struck with disbelief at my luck in finding him.

"Oh, no," the man chuckled. "Magic was locked away from this world many generations ago. It was too dangerous for humans to meddle with."

I frowned at him, confused. "Then what did you do?"

"Magic is not something concrete, Dagan," the man answered. "It is not like a pile of firewood or a herd of cows. It cannot simply be picked up and stuck in a shack. Some of it always seeps out."

"And you can use that…?"

"Yes. I know how to channel what little traces of it remain. It is not instant, as it would have been before. Each of us carries a small reservoir on our person. It is something we are all born with. Most people do not realize they have it. Even in the days when wild magic roamed free, only a select few would sense they had the capacity to capture it and unleash it to do their bidding.

"Now, it is much harder. It requires the utmost control of your mind. It requires immense concentration and willpower. It requires otherworldly persistence. But, if you can manage that," the man sat back, "you have the potential to become a God amongst men."

"Is that what you are?" I asked, my voice hushed.

He barked a laugh. "Hardly. But I do have more tricks up here," he tapped his head, "than most men discover in a lifetime."

"You'll teach me?" I asked, eager to learn. "You will, won't you? You wouldn't have told me all that if you didn't mean to."

"My, but you're a tenacious little brat," he said. He leaned across the table and ruffled my hair. "And I like your enthusiasm." His eyes glimmered. "Tell you what. If both of us survive the night, then I promise, I will teach you what I know."

CHAPTER SIXTEEN

I spent the rest of the day watching the man get more and more drunk.

In truth, his casual nonchalance made me uneasy. I saw what he could do: throw a knife. But, he'd done that when he was still sober. He said the Black Brotherhood was coming for him, but it was obvious that he did not see them as much of a threat.

It was either that, or he was insanely brave. Or stupid.

The thought seemed ironic. Those were the two qualities he'd identified in me earlier.

An hour after midnight, things became interesting.

I had been watching the tavern fill up with patrons as the evening progressed. The rundown bar was apparently a favorite spot of both nobility and peasants. You could distinguish each from the cut of his cloth. I had never seen the two types of people mingling together as freely as they did here.

The first customers who entered the bar after dinner eyed me curiously. I was an oddity. My presence didn't fit. But, the man I was with was still lucid enough to look intimidating, so I wasn't troubled.

However, I was worried that as he drank himself deeper into oblivion, somebody would take issue with my presence at Lamore's.

Instead, I found the opposite. As more people filled the space, I was given less and less attention.

A blue hen stands out in a flock of fifteen, but is lost in a crowd of one thousand.

Still, I jerked my head up every time I heard the front door open. I did not know how the Black Brotherhood would make their entrance, so every loud noise had the tendency to spook me.

A girl about my size, though probably at least ten years older, stood up on a table in the middle of the room with a harp. She strummed the strings and began to sing. The crowd joined her with the words of a song I did not know. It seemed to be a jolly melody.

The sound of the song made the man I was with perk up. He joined in. He sang with his full voice, slurring the words. When the song ended, he roared to his feet and cheered the loudest.

That was when I noticed two small men in brown, indistinctive cloaks walking toward us.

My eyes swept over them at first. They were so ordinary that nothing about them attracted attention. You could walk down the street and not notice their kind until you were a heartbeat away from a collision.

But, just as I was going to turn my attention back to the performance, the glint of a metallic edge in one man's hand caught my eye.

Everything seemed to happen at once.

The girl started to sing. Her song began with a chorus that everybody knew. A hundred voices burst to life around me.

At the same time, the men quickened their steps. Their faces showed absolutely no emotion, but their fingers danced. I saw blades twirling in their hands.

I screamed to alert the man. My voice was lost in the uproar.

One of the assassins swept both hands up. Silver flashed through the air.

The man I was with, the one who seemed so completely oblivious to his surroundings, lifted one arm. His wrist flickered.

Two knives that were aimed at his head fell listlessly to the floor.

I did not know who was more surprised by that: me, or the would-be assassin.

His companion scowled and leapt forward.

By then, the man I was with was already on his feet. He met the attacker head-on. They collided and fell to the ground.

I lost sight of them behind a table. Nobody in the crowd seemed to notice. I ran around, grabbing an empty metal mug out of somebody's hand. It wasn't much, but it felt better to be armed with something.

I skidded to a stop when I saw what had happened in that brief moment when I lost sight of the fight. The man in brown was lying on his back, dead. He had a knife lodged in his throat.

The man I was with turned toward me. His eyes widened in momentary surprise. Before I could react, two more blades appeared in his hands and hurtled through the air toward me.

They whistled by my ears. With a wet *thunk,* they landed into something solid. I spun around.

Not two feet away from me was a third attacker, also in brown. He croaked and fell, trying to stop the blood as it poured from his gut.

My heart was racing at this point—my body, flush with adrenaline.

The chorus started up a second time in the bar.

My companion turned and rolled forward as more knives flew at him. He lifted the body of the dead man and used it as a shield. The knives implanted into the brown-clothed chest.

It's funny the things your mind picks up in times like that. I realized, for example, that I did not know the man's name.

By then, the scuffle was beginning to attract attention. Two dead bodies will do that. Alarm rippled through the crowd.

The remaining attacker looked around, as if suddenly afraid to be seen. He reached inside his cloak and pulled out a small, round package about the size of a grapefruit. He threw it at his feet.

It exploded in a burst of smoke. People gasped and jumped away. When the smoke cleared, the man was gone.

"Dagan!"

My head whipped around. The man I knew motioned urgently to me.

I ran over. He gestured at the brown-cloaked body. "You can see him?"

"Of course."

"What does he look like?"

"Short hair, plain face. Large nose." I bent down and poked his shoulder. "Also dead."

The commotion had stirred most of the crowd. The song stopped. People were staring at us.

"Good observation," the man noted. He rose and strode for the door. "Come on."

I ran to catch up. A path formed in the crowd as people shuffled to get out of the way.

He opened the door and led me into the night. It was cold. A full moon hung amongst the stars. The man looked both ways, nodded to himself, and started quickly down the street. His gait reminded me of a wolf stalking its prey.

The man spoke as soon as I caught up to him. "Three attackers tonight, Dagan. You saw all of them?" He showed no signs of intoxication.

"Yes."

"Astounding," he muttered. "You could see them the same as you see me?"

"Yes!" I said. "What's so special about that? Anybody could!"

"No." He stopped mid-stride and turned toward me. He knelt down. His eyes were clouded with emotion. "Not anybody, Dagan. You were the only one in that room who could."

"What are you talking about?" I scoffed. "You *killed* them! You can't fight an invisible enemy!"

"I can," the man said. "Three assassins came from the Black Brotherhood tonight. They did not come in the flesh."

"I saw them," I repeated, incredulous.

"How many did I kill?"

"Two."

"And what happened to the third?"

"He… *disappeared.*" I choked on the word.

"You saw him do it?"

"He threw something that exploded at his feet. It sent off a bunch of smoke. Then, he was gone."

"How do you think he did that?"

I blinked. "I… I don't know."

"Do you want me to tell you why the Black Brotherhood is called the *Black* Brotherhood, Dagan?"

"Yes," I nodded.

"The Black Brotherhood is a cult that follows the teachings of Helosis. Helosis was a man—a leader amongst men—in the time before magic was sealed away. He was the most powerful human sorcerer the world has ever seen. His time was before even mighty Rel'ghar."

Seeing my confusion, the man continued. "Helosis was powerful, but discontent. He craved more than he had. He began dabbling in the dark arts. He intended to turn himself into a true God.

"Xune saw what Helosis was doing. He watched as Helosis corrupted the magics of the earth. He watched as Helosis turned them into something they were never meant to be.

"Xune was not threatened, for he knew he stood above all men. But he feared what would happen to those who attempted to channel the tainted elemental forces that Helosis was creating.

"Xune came down from his mountain and confronted the man. This was the moment Helosis was waiting for. He unleashed a great torrent of magic intended to destroy Xune.

"Xune laughed. The attack was as futile as a boy trying to break down the walls of a city with a willow stick.

"Yet his arrogance was misplaced. Helosis had command of forces even Xune did not know. Helosis struck Xune down.

"The god fell. Helosis commanded true power. But he reveled in his victory for too long.

"He could not control the forces he had unleashed. They grew stronger and stronger, swirling around him in a violent maelstrom of energy. Helosis grew frightened, for he had used the souls of the dead to power his crude, unnatural magic.

"Xune saw his chance. As Helosis struggled to contain the dark force, Xune spoke the words that would bind Helosis to his creation forever. Helosis screamed as the malevolent spirits feasted on him. And Xune, weary, reached out and touched Helosis to extract the final bit of life from his body.

"Helosis died on the spot. But Xune knew that even he could not contain the magic that had been created. It fled from the battleground and spread through the world like an infectious disease.

"Xune returned to his home, at ease. The threat had been soothed. He did not care for the residual magic, or the new dark forces that Helosis had birthed, so long as they could not be used against him. They were left to ravage humanity as they pleased.

"But when Xune left, he did not realize that Helosis had written treatises of his creations. Men found those pages years later. While none had the pure strength that Helosis commanded, they understood that a new force was present in the world.

"That, Dagan, was the birth of the Black Brotherhood. They are a cult that worships the dead. They call upon the magics that Helosis created to aid in their endeavors. Such unnatural power comes with a cost. All those in the Black Brotherhood forsake their souls. Each time they channel their power, they slip deeper into the realm of the dead, and lose their humanity.

"That's why you were the only one who could see the assassins. They reside in the shadow world, halfway between the living and the dead."

A cold shiver ran down my spine. "But, why can I see them? I'm not... *dead*, am I?"

"No, dear boy, you are *gifted*. Yours was not a regular birth." He glanced up at the rooftops. "We will speak of this later. For now..." His eyes trailed a line in the sky, "...we need to find the final assassin."

He took off down the street, his cloak billowing behind them. "But how can *you* see them?" I asked, running to keep up.

"Because, Dagan," the man glanced down, "I was once one of them."

CHAPTER SEVENTEEN

Together, we ran down the street.

"Does that mean only *I* can see you?" I asked. I knew the question made no sense: I saw the man interact with the coach driver, the bartender, and the whore. But I had to hear the answer from him to be sure.

"No," he said. He stopped, turned toward an alley, and stood at the entrance. I looked past him. It was dark.

"What do you see?" the man whispered.

"Nothing," I said.

"Look closer."

I peered past him. The high buildings on either side blocked out whatever moonlight seeped through the clouds. The alleyway ended in a raised wall. It was a dead end.

It seemed empty, at first. But then, the briefest flicker of movement caught my eye.

"There!" I exclaimed, pointing. "There's somebody in there!"

The man closed his eyes and inhaled deeply. "Yes," he said. "Yes, I can sense him too." He looked down at me. "Stay here, Dagan. If things get ugly, run."

"What are you going to do?"

The man grimaced. "I am going to finish the job I could not in the tavern."

Without another word, he strode into the alley. His wide shoulders and dark cloak cut an impressive figure in the night.

"Arretus," he called out. His voice rebounded off the narrow walls. "I know it is you, brother. Come out, and prove to me you are no coward!"

My breath caught as I waited.

Nothing happened.

"Arretus!" The man called again. "I know you are here. I can smell your rotting flesh. Show yourself! Reveal yourself to me!"

I caught a ripple of cloth in the air. I looked up, and saw the brown-cloaked man dropping from the rooftop.

"Watch out!" I screamed. "Above you!"

The man's head jerked up. He grunted as the one in the brown crashed onto his shoulders. They fell to the ground in a heap.

I heard the sounds of their struggle. Both men were vying for position over the other. The one in the black produced a knife, but had it knocked out of his hand before he could use it.

It skittered over the ground and came to a stop before me.

They were grappling now, rolling with each other in the dirt. They were both so close that neither could use his hands.

A cloud passed overhead, revealing the hidden moon. The blade of the forgotten knife shimmered in the night.

I looked up. The two men were evenly matched. Neither had the advantage. One single mistake could mean the difference between life and death.

I moved without thinking. I ran forward, swept up the knife, and leapt at the brown-cloaked man's back.

A memory flashed in my mind. Me, trying the same maneuver with Three-Grin. Doubt flared to life inside me. But, I had already committed.

I flew through the air and flinched just before I felt the knife sink deep into the man's back. For half a second, I'd expected him to spin around and counter the way Three-Grin had.

He could not. The man in the black demanded too much attention. I felt his muscles part as the blade bit home. The assassin arched up in sudden pain and surprise…

That gave the man on the ground the opening he need. A knife flourished in his hand and he cut across the brown-cloaked man's throat. Blood gushed out.

All in all, the whole sequence of events—from me screaming to alert the man, to right now—lasted less than the amount of time it takes to count to five. But to me, it felt as if hours had passed.

I fell back. The man kicked the body of his opponent off and came to his feet. Blood thundered in my ears. All I could hear past that was the sound of my raspy breathing.

My mind was blank. All I could process was that I had killed a man. I had *killed* a man.

"Dagan." The voice drew my attention. I looked up at the bearded man standing above me. His face and chest were a mask of red. "That was a brave thing you did." He paused. "But stupid."

I sputtered. "Stupid? I saved your life!"

"And risked your own. Acts like that will not keep you alive very long." He wiped the blood from his face with the sleeve of his coat.

"You could have died!" I countered.

The man raised an eyebrow. He kicked the body onto its back, and I saw, for the first time, two knives implanted into its chest.

He gestured to the blades. "Seconds before you came to the rescue," he deadpanned.

I blinked. "I... I didn't know."

"Clearly." He knelt down and pulled the knives out, then wiped them clean on the dead man's coat. He stood up and held out a hand toward me. "Come on. Times like these, a man could *really* use a drink."

Chapter Eighteen

I woke up the next morning in a room I did not remember. It smelled of tar and burnt wood.

A single window allowed light in. I blinked rapidly when I looked outside. It was so bright.

My head hurt. I did not know why. It felt a little like the days after the concussion I suffered at the hands of the two toughs in the gambling district.

"Ah, finally, Dagan is awake."

I turned toward the voice. The man was sitting in a chair, fully dressed, with a book in his lap.

"Where are we?" I asked.

He chuckled. "You don't remember? *Think*."

I tried. After the fight in the alley, the man led me to another dim tavern. This one had been empty. I remember him giving me a drink, and I recall scarfing it down, even as the liquid burned my throat.

I did not remember much after that.

"You're in my home," he reminded me gently. "At least, the place I call home for now. We're in an inn."

I scrubbed my eyes. "Why can't I remember?"

"That," he said as he flipped a page, "would be because you are sporting the very first hangover of your life. How does it feel?"

I tasted dry vomit on my tongue and cringed. "Like hell." Did I throw up?

The man laughed and stood. He poured a glass of water from a metal pitcher on a nearby vanity and handed it to me. "Hydrate. You'll feel better. Yesterday was your initiation into manhood."

"If this is what it feels like to be a man," I muttered, "I'd rather stay a kid."

That earned me a great guffaw of laughter.

I drank my water and felt my mind sharpen. I was caught by a flare of alarm as all of last night barreled into view.

"We just left him in the alley!" I exclaimed. "Won't somebody see the body?"

The man looked over his shoulder at me from the window. "Heh. No. Look at your hands."

I did. "What am I looking at?"

"Last night, your fingers were stained bright red," the man said. "You did not wash them. Where did the blood go?"

I looked up and shook my head. "I don't know."

"I told you that the Black Brotherhood exists in the place halfway between our world and the land of the dead. Do you remember that?"

I nodded.

"The men we fought left behind bodies on the cusp of both worlds. Without a life force holding them together, the bodies disintegrate in minutes."

My eyes widened. "So you're saying…"

"That the only thing left in the alley right now is a cloak with a few peculiar holes in it. Don't worry. Nobody will connect anything back to us."

I remembered something else he had told me last night. "You said you were one of them," I whispered. "Was that true?"

"Do I look like a man who would lie—especially after all I've revealed to you?" He grunted. "Yes. I was. Years ago."

"What happened? Why are you… not there… now?"

He clicked his tongue. "Ask too many questions, Dagan, and eventually the answers will get you hanged." He lowered his face to mine. "Do you understand?"

I understood that this was a prickly topic for him. So, I kept my mouth shut and nodded.

"Good. Now, come on. You'll have to show me where you used to live. We need to collect your things if you're going to train with me."

Chapter Nineteen

"Whoa, whoa there," Earl spoke. "You tellin' us that this man, this man who killed *three* of the Black Brotherhood, took you in under his wing? Just like that?"

Dagan nodded. "Yes. He, like the man who gave me the mark, saw me for who I was. Though at that point, I did not know who I was, myself."

"Your mother knew, didn't she?" Patch piped in. "That's why she tried to kill you."

"I told you my mother was wise. She knew."

"So what then?" Earl asked. "Who *are* you, Dagan? Some type of chosen one?"

The man in the hood barked a laugh. "No. That is not a privilege granted to one such as me."

Earl narrowed his eyes. "Who then?"

Dagan raised his gaze and matched Earl's. "I am the Damned," he said.

***

I showed the man the way to my home behind the crates. During our trip back, I finally learned his name.

Blackstone.

It was a fitting name for a man as mysterious as he. It was a name fitting for the powers he claimed to possess.

As we were leaving, I cast one last look over my shoulder at Magda's hut in the distance. Blackstone stopped and looked at me.

"Is there someone you want to see before we go, boy?"

"Yes," I said.

He nodded. "I will wait for you in the coach."

I ran all the way to her home, clutching all the coins I'd hoarded to my chest. I burst into her hut, but found it empty.

No. It was not *just* empty. It was not empty in the way a room is when it is free of people. It was empty in a more complete sense of the word.

It was empty the way a bar is empty after the last drop has been drunk and the last patron has left. It was empty in the way a mother's heart is empty after all her children have grown and left her care. It was empty the way your bed feels empty after the lover you've cherished has died.

Magda had left.

I did not know where she had gone. Some of her possessions were still on the walls, but more than half were missing. I had a feeling she did not intend to return.

Still, I walked to her bed and placed my meagre collection of coins under the pillow. Then, I plucked out one hair and laid it on top. That was the only way I knew to let her know the coins were from me.

I returned to the coach somewhat downcast. Blackstone sensed my mood, and did not make conversation. He told the driver to go, and we were off.

I did not know it then, but it would be the last time I saw south Hallengard for two years.

Later that day, we began my training.

Blackstone stood me in the middle of his room and told me to hold my arms wide. I did. Knives flashed. Before I knew it, my shirt fell in tatters to the floor.

"Speed," he told me, "is your greatest advantage. You don't need to be strong if you are quick." He flipped one knife over in his hand and poked my rib with the hilt. "And you, Dagan, are definitely not strong."

I grunted and took the insult.

He walked behind me and touched the scar on my collarbone. "How did you get this?"

"Knife," I said.

"No ordinary blade leaves a mark like that."

I shrugged. "It did for me."

I felt Blackstone nod. "Fine. Tell me, Dagan, how many blades do you think I carry?"

I thought on the question for a moment. I remembered last night, and counted all the knives I'd seen him produce. "Five," I said.

"Wrong. I have fifteen."

My face screwed up in disbelief and I turned my head back. "You don't have fifteen!"

"Eyes front!" he snapped. I whipped forward and stood straight.

"If you have fifteen," I said, not entirely comfortable having an armed man behind me while I did not have so much a shirt for protection, "where do you keep them?"

"If I told you, would you believe me? Or would you want to see for yourself?"

I considered the question.

"I'd need to see for myself," I said finally. I knew how easy it was to swindle people with words on the street.

"Good answer. I will let you. In time. But not in the way you think."

"Then how?" I asked, starting to turn back.

"Eyes forward, Dagan!" he growled.

I stopped and turned straight ahead.

"Do you trust me?" he asked.

"Not very much," I muttered.

He chuckled. "Liar. You trust me with your life. I'm going to prove it to you. Walk forward. Don't look back until I tell you to. Grip the two nails on the wall."

I did. The nails looked like they had been used to hang pictures, once. They were spread so far that I had to stretch to grip each one in my palm.

Something thudded into the wall by my right ear. I felt the reverberation of a blade. I started to turn my head toward it, when another *thud* sounded by my left ear.

I froze.

In a matter of seconds, I had knives outlining my entire body. The hairs on the back of my neck stood up.

I counted fourteen *thuds*. Blackstone spoke. "Step back."

I didn't move. "You forgot one."

"Did I?" he mused. "Step back and count."

I sighed, relenting, and did.

My mouth dropped when I saw that there were way more than fourteen knives in the wall. Double that, at least.

"I have two hands, Dagan," Blackstone said. "And I know how to use both. Also. Always let your enemy underestimate you. It gives you an advantage."

My mind spun with how I could have counted only fourteen thuds when, in truth, there were… *twenty-five, twenty-six, twenty-seven… twenty-eight* knives in the wall.

There was only one conclusion I could reach.

"You threw two knives at the same time," I marveled. The precision that must have taken was extraordinary. I looked over my bare upper body. There wasn't a knick anywhere.

"Yes," Blackstone said. I turned, and jumped in surprise when I saw a knife loping through the air, arcing toward me.

I sidestepped it to avoid getting cut.

"Next time, you catch that," Blackstone growled. "Pick it up and toss it to me."

I did. The knife spiraled through the air. Blackstone caught it in a flourish, and in the blink of an eye had it flying straight at me.

It whizzed an inch from my nose and imbedded itself in the middle of the outline on the wall.

Right where my head would have been.

I swallowed.

"In time," he said, "you will learn to do exactly that."

Chapter Twenty

If I had thought my life was hard before, I was wrong.

Blackstone was an uncompromising teacher. He was also a stark perfectionist. He expected me to obey him in anything he asked.

"Put your past life aside," he told me. "None of it matters now. Throw your old ideals and prejudices away. They will only hold you back. You've seen things, Dagan, that you thought would shape you. Nothing could be further from the truth. You are still young. To learn, you have to let me guide you. You must empty your mind and become a blank canvas for my words. You must be like wet clay: infinitely mendable in the hands of your master. Can you do that?"

"Yes," I said.

"You have to agree to go at the pace I set. No faster, and no slower. You must trust the method of learning and let your progress take its natural path. At times, you will want to push forward. At times, you will think I am working you too hard. You must keep those thoughts to yourself. Only I can gauge if you are learning at the proper speed. You cannot. Do you understand?"

"Yes," I said, impatiently. I was practically bouncing on my feet, ready to get started. "When will you teach me to use the knives?"

He struck me across the face. I fell and tasted blood.

"What was that for?" I demanded, angry.

"For lying. And for speaking out of turn. You pledged patience, yet the first words from your mouth betray your intentions. Did I make a mistake taking you in, Dagan?"

I swallowed my pride and forced my eyes down. "No."

"Good." Blackstone extended a hand to me and helped me up. His grip was strong as iron. "Do not lie to me again. It will not serve your purpose. The trust between a pupil and teacher is a delicate thing. I am giving you my time, and everything I know. In return, I ask you to follow directions. Will that be difficult?"

I bit my lip. "No," I said.

"Good. Will you ask about the knives again?"

"Only when you say I am ready."

A small smile crept onto Blackstone's face. "One thing you do have going for you, Dagan," he said, "is that you learn very fast."

***

I spent one year with Blackstone before he trusted me enough to hand me a blade.

It was a hard year. The hardest I have ever known. Blackstone would wake me at the first light of dawn and run me through his exercises until long after the sun had set.

He taught me that to control your mind, you must first control your body. My mind was alive and bursting with energy like a thunderstorm. My body was weak. Blackstone worked on that first.

He ran me to the bone. Each day began with a sprint to the river, where I would fill four buckets of water and carry them back on my shoulders. Blackstone timed each run. If I was slower than the day before, he would make me do it again. If I spilled a drop of water, he would make me do it again. If my shoulders weren't all the way up and my posture less than perfect when I returned, he would make me do it again.

That was the beginning of my physical training. It progressed from there. Four buckets became five. Five became six. Water became heavy, wet sand. And again, if I didn't at least match my previous time, Blackstone made me do it again.

He taught me something called the *Keta,* which was a lot like a slow-moving dance in a predetermined pattern. It was supposed to help clear my mind and teach me the limits of my body.

The *Keta* took two hours from start to finish. The first time I tried, my body was so exhausted that I collapsed into a trembling pile of sweat on the floor a quarter of the way through.

Blackstone rubbed ointment on my aching muscles and told me to start again. The second time, I collapsed even sooner.

His eyes darkened and he left the room. I found him hours later on the rooftop, smoking a pipe of tabac.

"Your lack of effort troubles me," he said when I approached. "I am starting to think this endeavor is a waste of my time."

He stood and left, leaving me to ponder his words.

The next day, I made it three-quarters of the way through the *Keta* before collapsing. I thought I was a failure. I expected him to kick me out on the spot.

But when Blackstone helped me up, he praised the perseverance I showed and told me that he knew I did not hold anything back.

Later that month, I learned that it took Blackstone six *weeks* of training before he got as far as I had on the second day.

We would spend three hours a day on mental training. Blackstone did not simply teach me facts to remember and recite. He gave me a much greater gift:

He taught me how to think.

Word and number riddles were his favorites. He quizzed me on them and then helped me discover the answers for myself. Nothing he asked required information I did not already possess, but some of the questions needed such elaborate twists of logic that they may as well have been spoken to me in a foreign language for the haplessness of the answers I gave.

Blackstone taught me to read, too. Whereas Magda let me go at my own pace, Blackstone pushed me like a slave driver. By the end of my tenure with him, not only had I read the classics—

from *Draconae* to *Gargolis*—but I could also recite any chapter from beginning to end by heart.

All in all, Blackstone kept me so busy that, when he told me a year had passed, I was astounded. All the days of tutelage seemed to blend together in my mind. It was one long, continuous journey with no breaks in between.

I could not even remember the seasons changing.

He tested at the end of the year. I was stronger. Quicker. My mind was sharper.

He had me grab a bar and pull myself up. When I began, I could not do it more than once. Now, thirty repetitions were easy.

My body was developing. I was growing. Even though I went to sleep exhausted each night, Blackstone fed me enough to recover.

For that, I was immensely thankful. There had never been a time in my life when food was not a scarcity. With proper nutrition, I flourished.

I also added a few much-needed inches to my frame. I was

becoming a man.

Chapter Twenty-One

Blackstone pulled a chair into the middle of the room and told me to sit. I did, and watched as he picked up a blackened twig from the fireplace and used the charred end to draw a circle around me.

"I told you before that there are multiple levels to your training," he said. He started a second circle, larger than the first. "The first ring represents the sum of the knowledge you had before you came to me." He tapped the second. "The next is all the knowledge you have accumulated in your time here."

He drew four more circles on the floor, for a total of six. "The area within each ring is a visualization of the knowledge you must gain to progress to the next level. As you can see, the gap between each ring gets larger and larger the farther you move out. Gaining the first level was easiest. Your task becomes more difficult as you progress.

"The first level took you one year. It was a decent pace. But, unless you want to spend the next decade of your life with me, I suggest you go faster."

"How?" I asked. "I do everything you tell me."

"Sometimes progress depends on more than just following direction, Dagan. Sometimes initiative is required."

I remembered his speech when we first began. "But you said—"

Blackstone held up one hand. "I know what I said. The things you tell a new initiate differ from what you tell one who has progressed."

I squinted my eyes at him, not quite understanding. "So, you're saying...?"

"I'm saying that I recall a boy who once wanted to learn the knives." A blade flashed in his hand, like a trout leaping from water. It was gone in the blink of an eye. "Now is the time to do that, Dagan."

Blackstone turned back and brought out a chest as large as I was. He dropped it on the table. Then, he opened the lid and motioned me over.

Inside were knives. Hundreds upon hundreds of knives. Some had blades no larger than my pinky. Others had metal blades that gleamed as long as my arm. Some had leather hilts, while others had hilts made of wood. Some blades had engravings on them, while others were completely bare.

"My humble collection," Blackstone said, with a knowing glimmer in his eye. "Take your pick."

I looked at him. "For what?"

"Choose a blade that catches your fancy." He nodded at the chest, then turned away. "Take your time. Make sure your selection is right for you."

I frowned at the knives as Blackstone left me alone. I hadn't the slightest idea how to pick.

There was a certain solemnity in Blackstone's words when he told me to choose. I suspected that my choice would reveal something about me.

I picked up the largest blade at first. The metal was twisted like a half-moon, but despite that, it was well-balanced.

I set it down. It did not feel right.

Next, I took out a long, thin blade that reminded me of a needle.

It did not feel right, either.

And so I went, on and on, picking up different knives and setting them aside. Each one I discarded made me more anxious about stretching out my decision for too long and displeasing Blackstone. But when I glanced over my shoulder, he was gone.

It was obvious he did not want me to feel pressured into choosing my blade. Even so, being alone only served to reinforce the importance of the decision.

I was not simply selecting a knife. I was selecting *my* knife.

And it had to be right.

So, I busied myself with looking through all of them. I didn't know what I was searching for. I just hoped, when I stumbled upon the right one, I would know.

I tried and discarded knives large and small. I tried and discarded ones with blades the width of my hand, and others as fine as pine needles. I tried ones that were big enough to be considered swords before setting them aside. I tried ones the same size as my old butter knife, before also setting them aside.

In the end, I narrowed my choice to three.

One was a silver blade with jewels encrusted in the hilt. I did not take it because I liked the sparkle. I took it because it was well-balanced and compact.

The second knife had a simple hilt and a long, dark blade. For someone my size, it was nearly a short sword. I chose it because it felt solid against my palm, and I could grip the hilt with two hands.

The third, and final, was an inconspicuous little thing that I had almost overlooked entirely. I did not even bother to pick it up when I first saw it. It looked too frail. But when my fingers brushed it by accident, I felt a tiny spark of power run up my arm.

The phenomenon did not repeat itself, no matter how many times I tried. I may have imagined it. Still, the experience stood out in the back of my mind. Maybe there was something special about the small knife.

I pulled up a chair and stared at the three choices before me. I felt as if the moment I picked one, my destiny would be sealed to it. It was not a decision I took lightly.

There was still no sign of Blackstone. I tried to think back and remember if he had ever given me any hints about this choice in my training.

I could not remember any.

So, I sat there, mulling over my choices, for long minutes that turned to hours. My hands hovered over each knife in turn, but I did not want to pick one up until I made my choice.

I weighed the pros and cons of each in my mind. But no matter how many times I went over my decision-making process, I could not help but feel that something was *missing*. Even though I had narrowed my selection to three, not one of them called to my heart.

I closed my eyes and took slow, deep breaths to clear my head of thought. That was one of the techniques Blackstone had taught me. He said it allowed you to transcend the limitations of your physical body and exist solely as a spirit in your mind.

I thought that was a crock of bullshit. But it did help me ease my nerves when I was stressed.

I opened my eyes. I noticed the light from outsider getting dimmer. I glanced over my shoulder, and saw the red sun dipping below the horizon. It was nearing dusk.

I turned back to the knives. Suddenly, a new feature of the chest caught my eye.

The lid was thrown back, and with the light shining in the room a particular way, I saw for the first time that the inside of the lid was padded.

I stood up and reached for it. My fingers traced the edges. I brought my free hand to the other side, and I felt that the lid was slightly thicker than it should be.

Aroused by curiosity, I pulled the chest toward me, disturbing the neat row of knives in front of it. I brought my ear to the inside of the lid and knocked.

It sounded hollow.

Excitement burst to life within me. I had discovered a hidden compartment!

I felt a flash of guilt at the same time. What if Blackstone didn't want me to know about it? But then, I figured if he trusted me enough to leave, he shouldn't get too angry if I found something I was not supposed to.

I flipped the chest over, so the lid was on the table, and started to search for my way in.

There was no button to push or lever to depress. All in all, the chest had the appearance of being solidly built.

But I knew that appearances were meant to deceive.

After searching every square inch of the surface for half an hour, I decided that the only way in would be to crack the inner lining.

Again, that tendril of guilt surfaced within me. Blackstone would be furious when he came back and found his chest ruined. I had no doubt of that.

He might even throw me out.

But, I was gripped by the curiosity that only a nine-year-old can feel. I thought that I had unearthed a great treasure. My mind buzzed with what I might find inside.

Most of all, it was fascination with the unknown that made me pick up the dark, thick knife, jam it into the side of the chest, and pull with all my might.

The chest cracked. I grinned and pulled harder. I hung my entire weight on the hilt and jerked it down.

I heard a splinter, followed by a loud *crack*. The blade torqued in my hand. I fell to the floor.

Quickly, I scrambled up, seized by the promise of seeing my discovery. When I laid my eyes on the inside of the chest, a murmur escaped my lips.

"Whoa."

Embedded within the surface I had broken were six knives of a kind I'd never seen before. Their blades were white like snow. Their hilts were yellow gold. Each had a slight curve along the neck of the blade.

My fingers shook as I reached out to pick one up. There was no doubt in my mind: Blackstone did not mean for me to find these knives. They were forbidden.

That made them so alluring.

I brushed the hilt with my fingers and sucked in a reverent breath. The metal was smooth and cold to the touch. I knew, just by looking at them, that these were no ordinary knives.

My fingers reached the blade. As soon as I touched it, a sharp, jolting pain exploded above my shoulder, right beneath the old scar on my collarbone.

Now, in the interest of full disclosure, I should say that at that precise moment in time, I did not know that my mother had been the one to give me that scar. I did not know that she had once tried to kill me. I did not know that I actually *had* seen a knife of this type before, when I was two.

I only learned those things years later, when I returned home and spoke to my mother minutes before her death.

Would she have died if I did not come and see her? No. But that is a story for another time.

Back in Blackstone's home, I cried out and jerked my hand away. Heat started to form around the scar. I felt it swarming down the length of my arm like an army of fireants, leaving a trail of menacing intensity.

I stumbled back. My foot caught the leg of the chair, and I fell. The heat was seeping into the very marrow of my bone. The pain was excruciating. I gritted my teeth and clutched my shoulder, hoping desperately that it would pass, and doing my best not to make a sound. I was terrified of how Blackstone would react if he saw me like this.

I rolled to all fours and tried to push myself up. But as soon as I put the smallest amount of weight on that arm, the pain magnified ten-fold. It felt as if an inferno had opened and swallowed my shoulder whole. I opened my mouth to scream, but by then the pain was too much, and my body was too far gone.

I passed out from shock.

CHAPTER TWENTY-TWO

I came to, shivering from the cold, even though I was under a pile of blankets. A wet rag lay on my forehead.

I was drenched in sweat. I lifted my head to look around, and that slight movement sent a piercing pain through my head.

I saw movement flicker in the corner of my vision. I turned my eyes that way and found Blackstone.

He looked exhausted. His irises floated in a sea of red. His eyes were rimmed by dark circles. His hair was unkempt, his usually tidy beard disheveled. His shirt was creased in many places, as if he'd been sleeping in it for days.

"Here," he said, giving me a full cup. "Drink." His voice was hoarse and heavy.

I took the wooden cup from him and winced as I sat up. Motion of any kind disturbed the uneasy equilibrium my body had adopted.

I drank the liquid—not water—under Blackstone's watchful eye. It burned my throat. It tasted of pinesap and alcohol. When I was done, I tried to give the cup back to Blackstone. He grunted and ignored my outstretched arm.

Suddenly, I remembered the chest. If I was in bed, and Blackstone with me, he must have seen what I'd done!

"I'm sorry," I began, "I didn't—"

"Drop it." Blackstone's command left no room for argument. "Don't tell me you're sorry unless you mean it. I know you don't. Because you don't even know what you should be apologizing for."

"Your chest," I said. "I broke it open."

He barked a hard laugh. "You think I'm worried about some piece of wood? No." He glowered down at me. "I should have expected you to be curious enough to investigate what's hidden inside. That, I do not fault you for."

"Then what?" I asked.

"Do you remember what happened to you *after* you broke into the chest, Dagan?"

I thought back. "I... I touched the hilt of one of those white knives. And then, when my fingers brushed the blade..."

"You awoke the power latent in it," he finished for me.

I stared at him. "What?"

"Look at your left shoulder."

I turned my head away from him and looked. My eyes widened when I saw the scar on my collarbone. It pulsed a vile red, almost like a living thing. The skin around it was marred black with corruption.

"That is your body trying to fight." Blackstone picked up a wrapped package off the floor. He set it down on the bed and carefully unrolled the cloth.

A single ivory knife lay inside.

I sucked in a breath that shot another jolt of pain through my head. The blade was *glowing*. A red aura surrounded it like a small, foggy haze.

"This is the knife you touched, Dagan," Blackstone said. "Your body activated it, and you bound yourself to it the moment the connection was made."

He put his hands beneath the cloth and offered the knife to me. "Take it. It is yours."

I looked at him warily without moving. The last time I touched the knife, pain exploded at my shoulder and I passed out. Why would things be different now?

Blackstone saw my hesitation. "It won't hurt you this time," he said. He motioned to a small table beside the bed.

I turned my attention to it. There was a white, porcelain plate in the middle. It had a single sliver of white ivory on it, coated in blood.

I saw the operating tools beside it. An iron needle. A spool of thread. Tweezers.

I looked back at my shoulder, and saw the tiny stitches marching over my scar.

"I pulled that out of you," Blackstone said, nodding to the bloody plate. "It's a fragment of a knife like this one."

I didn't know why I had a fragment of a knife inside me. And I had no idea why Blackstone had to take it out. "What are they?" I asked.

"The white knives are blades inlaid with old magic. Once, they were aplenty in the world. Hundreds. Perhaps thousands. They were prized because they were light as a feather. They did not dull.

"In the dark years after Rel'ghar fell, knives like these became feared. All relics of magic were feared. They were gathered and destroyed. Kings paid ransoms for them quadruple their weight in gold. The goal was to restore mankind to normalcy by eliminating all traces of magic from the world.

"But some who owned the knives hoarded them. The unlucky ones were found and killed. Their families were burned at the stake for permitting evil to linger.

"Eventually, only twenty such knives remained. Two were given to each of the ten noble families for protection. The families vowed to keep them safe."

"But you have *six*," I marveled. "How?"

"I told you the Black Brotherhood is mostly a band of thieves," Blackstone said. "They possess more magical remnants than any other group in the world. They are the only ones who practice magic openly, although they cannot do very much. I got the six from them."

"You *stole* them," I said.

"I did not steal them." Blackstone looked down at me. "I retrieved them. Once they were in my possession, I had no need of the Black Brotherhood anymore."

***

Blackstone explained to me that the moment I touched the ivory knife in his chest, the power in it clashed with the sliver that was in my shoulder. Each knife had a certain blend of magic. My body was rejecting the bit of it inside. That was why I passed out.

I found out I'd been asleep for seven days. Blackstone was not a healer. He hired an old woman to look after me until my fever broke. She left the day that happened. I awoke forty-eight hours later.

I wondered if she might have been Magda. I remembered the thing she told me when I first awoke in her hut: that she knew people who could teach me.

Was it just coincidence that I came under Blackstone's protection? Or did *she* arrange it? Was that the reason she was gone when I tried to find her a year ago? To give me a clean break from her, so I could fully commit to training with Blackstone?

I did not know for sure. But I suspected the truth lay somewhere along those lines.

Blackstone resumed my training as soon as I could stand. After the accident, he expected twice as much from me to make up for the time I'd missed.

I am proud to say that I delivered.

The ivory knife never left my side. As soon as I gripped it on that bed, I felt a new power seep into me. It gave me strength. Blackstone said that was the bond forming between me and the weapon.

Apparently my body, through no effort of my own, was highly attuned to magic. So much so that even the remnants of the spell left on the knife energized me.

That was my great gift. That was what my mother feared, and that was the reason she tried to kill me. That is why I could see the Black Brotherhood assassins when nobody else could.

Blackstone was not as gifted as I was. But he was trained by them. He knew Helosis's power and teachings. That is how he fought invisible foes.

My ability did not seem like such an amazing thing to me at the time. With most of the world's magic sealed away, there was little I could do with it.

The glow around the blade lessened each day. It disappeared entirely after a month. So did the energy I felt when I held it.

Blackstone told me I'd developed a kind of tolerance. The power the knife contained was still there. It simply affected me less.

That was the entire extent of the benefit of magic.

Nonetheless, I treasured that blade. It was light and could cut through anything. It never dulled and required no sharpening. It could not be broken.

Or so I was told. My mother's experience proved different.

Blackstone taught me how to use it as a weapon. He taught me the seven points of the human body that are most vulnerable. He taught me how to move with the blade as one.

Soon, holding it felt as natural as having fingers. It became an extension of my arm.

Blackstone also gave me smaller throwing knives. He taught me how to conceal them so they did not stand out in regular clothes, but, at the same time, were always accessible. He taught me the importance of balance and speed.

Don't get me wrong. Training was not a walk in the park. I had more cuts on my hands from handling the blades after a week than all the gnashes I'd received over my lifetime combined. After a day of throwing, both shoulders throbbed. The scar that Blackstone opened never fully healed. It affected my left arm. I had to learn to counteract the difference to perfect my aim.

Blackstone seemed pleased with my progress. Two months after we started again, he sat me down and told me how well my skill was developing. He said that, if I continued at my pace, in half a year he would send me out into the outside world.

The idea thrilled me. I did not know what he expected, but I was ready to show him anything he wanted to see.

One day at supper, he asked me a question I was not ready for.

"Dagan," he said, "do you know how I can afford you?"

I took a bite of the chicken thigh I was holding. "I thought you were rich."

He blinked, then laughed. "No. But I know of ways to make myself rich—at least, temporarily."

"How?"

"There are things I learned in the Black Brotherhood."

"You mean, stealing?" I took another bite.

He nodded. "Aye, stealing. Stealing and thievery and all those elaborate schemes of improving one's position in life. My last heist came two weeks before I met you. We've been living off that since, but the well's starting to run dry. You aren't cheap to clothe or feed. You have the appetite of three grown men."

I took that as a sort of veiled compliment and allowed myself a smug smile.

"I don't steal from just anybody, Dagan," he said. "Never from the poor. Rarely from the rich. My thefts are from the corrupt. I take back the things that were never rightfully theirs."

"Do you return those things to the people they took it from?" I asked.

He laughed. "No. I'm not a bloody priest."

"Oh."

"I'm telling you this because I want to know if you have any problems with it. I know some grow up believing stealing is wrong."

I shook my head. "No problem," I said. Thievery was the one thing I was good at before I met Blackstone.

"Good," he said. "I have another heist planned. Tomorrow, we begin training for it."

Chapter Twenty-Three

Blackstone woke me earlier than usual the next day. He threw a ragged collection of clothes on my bed. "Put those on."

I held them out. There was a pair of brown, patchy pants and a soiled, scratchy, wool shirt. They were worse than the clothes I'd worn when I lived on the street.

I knew better than to ask irrelevant questions, so I changed into them without a word.

Blackstone was dressed completely the opposite of me. His rich, green jacket had embroidery all over the front. The sleeves ended in bits of lace. He had a crisp, white shirt underneath and pressed pants.

He'd also trimmed his beard so that it was no more than a dark shadow.

"Today, you observe," he told me. "You do not speak to anyone. Only watch."

I nodded in agreement.

"You'll trail after me on the rooftops," Blackstone said. "I remember you had some capacity for that before, no?"

"Yes," I said. I hadn't scampered up walls and on tops of buildings since Blackstone took me in, but I doubted my skills could have eroded. If anything, I was quicker and more agile now. I was better suited for following him unseen.

He clapped his hands together and told me to get up. I did.

Blackstone left the house first. He told me to count to sixty before following.

I got impatient and ran out at forty-one.

The street, as expected, was mostly empty this early. I looked at the outer facades for a way to the roofs. I found my path in a low window.

I caught my foot on the windowsill and pushed up. My hands wrapped around a rain pipe for support. One strong lunge had me gripping the edge of the roof. I pulled myself up.

Standing straight, I looked around for Blackstone. I spotted a man in a green jacket hurrying away from the house. I ran after him.

I did not know where he was leading me, but I ran along the rooftop like a shadow. My steps were light and made little noise. I stayed close enough to never lose sight of him, but far enough to remain unseen.

All in all, I thought I was doing quite well.

Until I felt an ice cold blade slip in front of my throat.

"One move and I gut you," a voice rasped in my ear.

All the training I had learned rushed to mind. Like Blackstone taught, I tucked my chin, trapping the blade. My arm shot out to dislodge the assailant's grip. I felt the blow connect, and was just about to duck and roll, carrying the blade with me, when a hand tangled in my hair and stopped me.

"Nice try," the voice hissed. "But you're too slow. Whoever taught you should be ashamed."

Panic exploded in my chest. It lasted only the length of time it took for me to hear the laughter at my ear.

The knife fell away. I sputtered when I turned and saw Blackstone.

He was wearing the same rags as I was.

"But, but you're supposed to be over there!" I complained, waving my hand toward the man moving along the street.

"You use your eyes, but you do not see," Blackstone said. He gestured toward the same shape. "Look at the way his shoulders lurch when he walks. Have you ever seen me move that way?"

I looked at the man below us again. I saw the nervous tightness in his neck, like he expected an attack at any moment. I saw the slight limp in his step that I had missed before.

"Dammit, you told me to follow you, and that's what I was doing!" I cried out.

"No. You were following the green jacket. Not me."

My cheeks burned. I'd fallen for his decoy. "That's not *fair*," I pouted.

"Life isn't fair, Dagan. The streets aren't fair. They will swallow you whole before you get your feet on the ground if you don't watch what you're doing."

"I don't understand," I said. "When did you have time to change? How did you get behind me?"

He scoffed. "You were so focused on the green jacket that you forgot to watch your surroundings. What did I teach you?"

"*He who closes his eyes is dead*," I recited by rote.

"Correct. And you never even opened them this morning."

I looked down at my feet.

Blackstone clicked his tongue. "Oh, stop looking so dejected. Everybody falls for a trick like this their first time. It's what you learn from it that shapes who you become."

CHAPTER TWENTY-FOUR

After I learned to follow Blackstone without losing him, we began new exercises.

We would start each morning in the heart of the merchant district of north Hallengard. The plaza began filling up with people from the first rays of the sun. It was busy until long after sundown.

Blackstone would pick a person at random and slip a small item in their pocket. Sometimes it was a worthless jewel. Other times, a coin. Yet other times, a simple rock.

It was up to me to follow that person and get the item back.

It was an exercise in caution and patience. I had to wait for the perfect moment to strike. Since I was doing it in the daytime, I did not have the luxury of blending in with the shadows, as I'd done before when I was on my own.

It was not easy. With so many eyes around you, discretion was the most important virtue. I was not always successful. Sometimes, the person disappeared before I had a chance to get close. Other times, I hesitated a second too long, or went a heartbeat too soon, and had to stop before I could even stick my hand in his pocket.

Progress was slow. My excitement about finally being let outside quickly faded. Blackstone gave me little feedback. In fact, he had grown uncharacteristically quiet. I was not sure how to take his shift in mood.

After two months of practice, however, I was getting better. My successes were not guaranteed, but nine times out of ten I did manage to get the item back.

There was no further mention of the heist that Blackstone told me about. I did not ask him about it, either. I figured that he thought I was simply not yet ready to take the next step.

The third month, an event occurred that changed my life forever.

It was a day like any other. Blackstone had woken me early and we walked to the plaza. That day, I was trailing an elderly gentleman with greying hair and the air of an aristocrat.

My job appeared to be easy at the start. The target did not seem particularly aware of his surroundings. Yet, every time I got close, a peculiar prickle in the back of my mind stopped me from acting.

It was the uncomfortable feeling of being watched. While I knew Blackstone kept an eye on me at all times, this was different.

I trusted that feeling. Sometimes, your unconscious mind is able to pick up cues that your waking mind might not. Something was not quite right. I began to suspect the man I was trailing was more dangerous than I first thought.

I followed him like a shadow as he made his way through the city. Oftentimes, he stopped to greet a passing friend. Conversation was always quick, and those were the moments I thought I should make my move. If I waited too long, I knew, the man might eventually disappear into a building—his home, for example—and not come out for hours.

That scenario presented a set of circumstances that I was not eager to explore. Breaking into a house is a lot different from pickpocketing somebody. For one, there was the front door. Blackstone had taught me to open locks. I had a pretty good hang of it, and could already do three-tumbler pins in under a minute.

Sometimes, breaking into a home could be easier, because a good thief knew to enter only if the place was unoccupied. Yet the anxiety of not knowing exactly how long you had before the occupants returned wreaked havoc on your nerves.

Nonetheless, every time I came close to the man, that prickling feeling intensified, and I was forced to stay my hand.

I followed him for hours. By appearance, I thought he might be a banker. I saw the heavy coin purse on his belt. I knew that it was just a distraction. He would have notes of tender on him, carefully concealed in his inside pockets. They were each worth three or four times the amount in his purse even if every coin were gold.

Eventually, he made his way to a reputable-looking tavern. I couldn't get in through the front door—not in my clothes—but I wasn't about to give up.

I circled the building once, looking for an alternate way in. I found it in the back. It was not the backdoor where deliveries were made and garbage was thrown out, but higher, above that: a small, diamond-shaped window leading to the attic.

A pair of men—probably cooks, by the flour on their aprons— gave me curious looks when they saw me in the back alley. I didn't want to give them reason to get suspicious, so I kept my head down and walked past. I stopped on the other side of the corner and waited. When I heard them head inside, I turned back.

I climbed onto a stack of barrels, jumped to reach the edge of the roof, and pulled myself up. I walked over to the window, which was a foot or so below me. It'd be awkward to get into, but not impossible.

I hung down over the ledge and used my toe to push at the window. It was unlocked. My foot found the windowsill and I dropped inside.

A babble of voices greeted me. The tavern had an open design with thick oak beams running across the ceiling. I could see the whole layout from my perch.

I looked around and found the grey-haired banker in one corner. His eyes kept darting around the room. He tapped his fingers against the table in a quick, nervous, *tat-tat-tat-tat*.

To my disappointment, he'd left his jacket on. It would have been much easier to retrieve Blackstone's coin if the man had hung it up.

Of course, I knew by now that I could not expect things to be so easy.

I balanced myself on the largest beam and started to creep across. I stayed low and moved slowly. I could not risk attracting attention by rushing over and making.

I was halfway to my destination when the sound of one particular voice stopped me in my tracks. It rose above the others and was immediately distinctive to my ears.

Three-Grin's voice.

A cold chill ran down my back. I looked below and saw him.

He was moving through the bar with an entourage of six men. He walked with a cocky strut, towering a head taller than anybody else. His voice was loud and rude as he called out for drinks.

I saw the banker straighten as Three-Grin approached him.

A painful cramp shot through my hand. I looked down and discovered that I'd unconsciously started gripping the hilt of my ivory knife.

Hard.

I eased my fingers loose and did not dare move as my eyes followed Three-Grin.

He walked toward the banker and sat down at the table with a crash. The men who came with him formed a formidable wall, cutting off access to that corner to the rest of the patrons.

Five running steps and a silent leap had me on a nearby beam that positioned me right above their table.

"What we're doing for you," the banker's voice filtered up to me, "is highly suspect. The contents we're moving around are attracting attention. People are starting to ask questions."

"Deal with it," Three-Grin growled. "I don't pay you to complain. I pay you to care for my investments."

The other man swallowed. "Yes. About that. You see..."

Three-Grin leaned close. "You wouldn't be suggesting that you're having... *problems*?" There was an undeniable threat held in the final word.

"No, no, not problems exactly," the banker corrected quickly. He tugged on the neck of his shirt. "It's just... more difficult than we expected. Moving that type of cargo around the city arouses curiosity, and curiosity turns to rumor, which filters up to the city guard..."

"Then make sure it doesn't," Three-Grin hissed. "Because if you fail me... Xune will know."

The other man started stammering placating words. I stopped listening. My fingers hovered over the sheaths of my throwing knives.

Blackstone forbade me from using those knives unless my life was at risk. He made me swear an oath that I would use them only in case of life or death.

I pulled one out and idly ran my thumb over the edge.

Three-Grin was completely vulnerable. I burned with hatred for him. The six men who came with him ensured that nobody approached from within the pub. They did not protect him from enemies above.

All it would take was one well-aimed throw, and the monster who defined my childhood would finally be dead.

Or would he? I remembered the uncanny way he sensed my last attack against him. Three-Grin was a large man, and I was still a boy. Hearing his voice brought me back to all the times I had hidden when I heard him approach. I remembered his drunken ramblings, and the way he killed for *pleasure.*

Would one knife be enough? Could I trust myself to throw the blade straight and true?

I saw his heavily-muscled neck. My throw had to be absolutely perfect if I intended to kill him. And after, could I get out in time?

I glanced back the way I came. The window was far—too far for me to make a quick exit. The moment the knife left my hand, everybody would know where it came from.

I would not escape.

That was the reasoning that ran through my head as I perched on the beam, still as a statue. You would think that logic would be enough to convince me not to strike.

But logic was secondary to the strength of my hatred for the man. I hated Three-Grin for what he did to his daughters. I hated him for what he did to his slaves. I hated him for who he was and what he represented.

I wanted revenge for Alicia. That feeling had subdued somewhat in the nearly two years I'd spent with Blackstone, but seeing Three-Grin again rekindled it with a searing passion.

I wanted revenge *now*.

If I could take this monster out of the world, my ambitions would be complete. Perhaps it didn't matter if I did not escape. Perhaps this was what I was meant to do.

Maybe, just maybe, this was fate's way of ensuring that my life could mean something.

If I attacked Three-Grin, I would die. I saw the crossbows slung across the shoulders of two of his guards. As soon as the knife left my hand, they would look up, see me, and fire…

But maybe I would be redeemed in death. It would be a glorious way to go.

I took another throwing knife out of its sheath. My eyes focused on Three-Grin's bulging neck. Two knives. Two chances. If I could sever his spinal cord—

My thoughts were interrupted when a commotion rose amongst the men standing guard.

Quickly, I pressed myself to a vertical beam. Then, I tilted my head and peered down.

There was a seventh man in the group. A drunk, if his lurching movements were any indication. He wore a hood so I could not see his face.

He was trying to break through the human wall and get to Three-Grin and the banker.

"Hoy!" he called out. "Hoy, it's me, Johnny! Don't you remember me? Johnny!"

Three-Grin turned back and shot a disgusted look at the man. He flipped his hand, and one of the guards pushed Johnny down.

He stumbled and fell. His hood dropped from his head. I saw his face, and an immediate tightness exploded in my chest.

It was Blackstone.

His eyes darted up to me at that moment. I saw, for the flicker of a second that our gazes crossed, that he was fully lucid.

Then he resumed his act.

"It's me! You don't remember Johnny?" He stood and stumbled forward again, straight into the arms of one of the guards. "Johnny. *Johnny*! I was your best fighter."

Again, he was pushed away. One of the guards drew his sword. "You take another step, you useless drunk, and you're a dead man."

Johnny-slash-Blackstone held up his hands, affronted. "All right, all right," he said, backing off. "No need to get violent, now."

"Piss off," the guard spat.

By then, the confrontation had attracted the attention of the entire tavern. The owner ran over, trailed by three guards of his own.

The hairs on the back of my neck stood up. I felt like a twig in a dry forest in the middle of the summer heat. The smallest spark would start an enormous conflagration.

"You," the owner scowled at Blackstone, "get out of here." He eyed Three-Grin and his entourage. "And you, sirs, I will have to ask to leave. Finish your drinks and go. I will not have you threatening my customers."

Three-Grin roared to his feet. He was still as imposing as ever. The scars on his face twisted as he sneered in anger.

The owner did not back down. "I said," he repeated, "that you are going to have to leave."

"I heard what you said," Three-Grin barked. He picked up his ale and chugged it down in a deliberate, angry swallow. He slammed the mug back on the table and wiped away the foam off his lips with one livid stroke of his hand.

"Piss on your bar," he said, "and piss on you. Can't even bloody serve drink that don't taste like watered down goat's milk."

He stepped forward and addressed the men around him. "Let's get out of here." He gave a mock bow to the owner. "Obviously, we're not *high class* enough for his establishment."

Some of his friends snickered. He strode away, and they followed him in a bunch. All except the grey-haired man.

Only when Three-Grin slammed the door did the banker exhale a breath as heavy as his last and sag down.

CHAPTER TWENTY-FIVE

"What the hell was that?" I practically screeched at Blackstone when I met him outside. "What were you doing in there?"

"Protecting *you*." Blackstone shot me a hard look. "Did you forget your task?"

"No, I was going to—"

I cut off as a glimmer of metal flew from Blackstone's hand to me in an arc. I caught it and looked in my palm.

It was the coin I was supposed to retrieve.

"How did you get this?" I stammered. "You didn't even get close to the man *once*!"

"A thief must be quick, Dagan," he said, "but an assassin, invisible. You were neither today."

I gritted my teeth in frustration. "That's not what I asked!"

Blackstone turned on me. "That's the answer you get."

I stared back at him, meeting his challenge head-on. The standoff lasted only a second before I relented and looked down.

It was the longest I'd ever defied Blackstone .

"You were asked to get that coin back," Blackstone continued, his voice filled with anger, "not try to kill a man."

I sputtered, flabbergasted. "I didn't—"

"You *did*." Blackstone's voice left no room for argument. "If I hadn't stepped in, you would have. Don't lie to me."

"I was waiting for the moment to get the coin back!" I defended. "I would still be in there, if you didn't interrupt!"

"Oh no," Blackstone said. "If I hadn't interrupted, you would be a cold body on the floor of that pub with half a dozen crossbow bolts stuck through you."

"I wouldn't—"

"You *would*." Blackstone flashed his eyes at me. "You think you're smart, Dagan. You think that just because I've given you two years of training you're better than others. You've made progress. I don't deny that. But you remain transparent in your desires. I saw the look in your eyes when you were crouched by the roof. You meant to kill."

"I—"

"Do you deny it?" His hard voice cracked like a boulder fracturing. "Will you look into my eyes and tell me you truly did not intend to kill anybody today?"

I looked at Blackstone. There was an unnerving undercurrent of danger to his words. If I lied, I had a feeling he would see right through it.

I averted my eyes. "I may have thought about it," I admitted.

"*Thought about it,*" he repeated, dissatisfied. "Hah! You had the look of a wild hyena circling its dying prey. If you believe you were *just* thinking about it, than you are more lost than I imagined."

"I *wanted* to kill him," I said. "I know what you told me about not using the knives. But you don't know who that man is! You don't know what he did to me."

"Dagan." Blackstone stopped and went down to one knee. He stared deep into my eyes. "I know Three-Grin."

"What? You do? How?"

"I know," he said, "because I was the only one of his slaves to survive the Arena."

CHAPTER TWENTY-SIX

My mind spun. My world seemed like it would collapse on itself at any moment.

"*You* were one of Three-Grin's slaves?"

Blackstone nodded once. "Yes. I was raised a slave, like you. Back then, the man you wanted to kill was not yet known as Three-Grin. But he was my master nonetheless."

"And you *escaped*?" I marveled. "How?" Before he could answer, another thought occurred to me. I never told Blackstone about Three-Grin. "How did you know *I* was a slave?"

"I can put enough pieces of your past together. Did you think I truly took you in without knowing a thing about you?"

I shook my head. "I... I don't know."

"No, Dagan. I know who you are. I know what you've been through. And I know that you want revenge."

The explanation made no sense. "Then why did you *stop me*?"

"Because you are not ready. You are too young. You are like a wolf cub come across his first wildcat. You saw the pack take one out many times as you grew. You are bold. Rash. You fancy yourself courageous. You jump to attack, thinking you'll be successful, never thinking about the consequences if you are not…

"Listen to me, Dagan. Revenge is like a poison. It seeps through your heart. It takes hold of you and possesses you to do stupid, reckless things. It is a fiery emotion that scorches away any wisp of common sense. It's powerful. It cannot be ignored. I am not asking you to try. I am *telling* you that you must recognize it for what it is. You have to control it. You have to possess it. You cannot let it possess you."

"I could have done it," I said quietly. "I could have killed Three-Grin. You taught me enough. You know it's true."

"Yes, but I did not teach you to throw your life away. You must be smart with these things. You cannot act the first chance you get without thinking about what happens after."

"But now he's *gone*," I said. "I'll never get a chance again!"

"That does not have to be true."

"What do you mean?" I asked. I furrowed my brows at him. "And what about you? Don't *you* want revenge, too? You could have killed Three-Grin in there. I know you could have!"

Blackstone smirked. "Yes, I could have. But that would be me acting on my emotions. It would be rushing forward without a plan."

"You would get away, though," I say. "You *know* how to kill. Why didn't you?"

"Because, Dagan," Blackstone said, "Three-Grin is not the true evil you think he is. I could kill him, but another would sprout up and take his place. We are not vigilantes. I told you this before. We are thieves."

He stood up. "And tonight, we are going for the greatest prize of all.

"The Arena."

***

That day, I learned from Blackstone what the Arena truly was.

It is a betting ring. Children are the fighters. It existed in the corrupt underbelly of Hallengard. It existed in a place known as the Hells.

Men with a thirst for blood placed enormous bets on the fighters. There were many slavers on the outskirts of Hallengard who tried to raise children for the Arena. Four dominated the rest.

Three-Grin was one of them. The others were Boar-Face, Wolf-Moon, and Cattle-Prod.

They all adopted different names to hide their identities. Despite my hatred for Three-Grin, I thought his was the best.

For the past five years, Three-Grin's children have been dominating the Arena. He was heralded as the best in the world.

Three-Grin got a cut of all his winnings. The slavers were not permitted to place pets directly to prevent collusion. But, they were allowed a certain percentage every time one of their fighters won.

For the combatants, there was no such thing as a victory. Every fight was to the death. Sure, some survived longer than others. But, in the end, all succumbed to the vicious cycle that claimed their lives.

Except, apparently, for Blackstone.

He told me he had won sixteen fights—a number unheard of. The record before him stood at eight.

Someone from the Black Brotherhood saw him fight, and paid a king's ransom for his release. The Brotherhood took him in and trained him. Blackstone would not elaborate on what that entailed—no matter how hard I pressed.

I learned all that as he and I rode back to his home to prepare.

Three-Grin was in town to watch a flagship fight. It was happening two days from now. Word on the street was that the current champion had a chance to overtake the boy who had survived twenty years ago.

His winning streak stood at fifteen.

"Dagan," Blackstone told me, "things are going to be dangerous. When we go in there, one of us might die. Perhaps we both will.

Nobody has tried to infiltrate the Arena like this in the past. This might be the only chance we get."

"How do we get in?" I asked.

"That's the easy part." Blackstone grinned. "You pretend to be a deaf mute. I pretend to be your slaver. The flagship fight occurs last. There will be plenty of smaller ones beforehand to warm up the crowd. It gives them a thirst for blood."

"You're going to enter me in the fights?" I asked.

"Yes. But we're going to rig the place first." He tossed a small, round bundle at me.

There was a tiny glass orb with a black, grainy powder inside. A bit of string came out of one end.

"What is this?" I asked.

"A fire starter. Light the wick, and the orb explodes."

"Like what I saw the assassin use?" I asked, thinking back two years when I first met Blackstone.

"Yes," he said, "but much more powerful. You hold in your hands enough power to destroy this entire room."

I looked up at him, incredulous. *This innocent-looking glass orb?* I thought.

"Is it magic?" I asked.

"No," he said. "It's science. Come." He beckoned me around back. "Look at this."

I found a wagon loaded with six barrels behind his house. It had not been there that morning.

"Delivered a few hours ago," Blackstone said, tapping one of the barrels. He jumped up and bid me to follow.

I climbed after him, and was immediately struck by the smell. The barrels emitted a foul odor reminiscent of dry manure, but with a sharp, metallic tang underneath.

Blackstone lifted one of the barrel tops. I looked inside. It was filled with the same black powder I had seen in the orb.

I reached out and picked up a handful, then let the fine grains fall through my fingers. The powder stained my hand black.

"They're *all* like that?" I asked, motioning at the other five barrels.

"Yes," Blackstone said.

"And the orb you showed me can *really* destroy a room?"

Blackstone eyed me. "You don't believe me." He took out a match from his pocket. "Would you like a demonstration?"

I nodded.

"Not here," he said. He closed the barrel lid and stepped down. I followed him as he strode out of his backyard, into the street.

"Where?" I asked.

"The river."

I followed Blackstone to the water. We waited until there was nobody around, then walked to the highest point of the bridge.

Blackstone looked down at me. I met his eyes. He reached into his pocket and produced a match, then lit the wick coming out of the small glass orb.

He extended his arm back and threw the orb as far as he could downriver.

It landed in the distance with a small splash, swallowed by the current.

"Just wait..." Blackstone murmured.

Out of nowhere, an explosion made water burst up like a giant geyser. It combined with a sound like crashing thunder that rocked the bridge.

Then all was quiet. I stood gaping, gripping the side of the bridge tight. If a tiny glass orb could do all that...

"What are you going to do with all the barrels?" I asked when we turned back.

"You mean, you still haven't figured it out?" Blackstone paused.

"We are going to blow up the Arena."

***

That night, under cover of darkness, we made our first move.

The plan was simple: sneak the loaded barrels into the Arena. Place them in strategic locations underneath the structure. The night of the big fight, start a fire that would evacuate the place. Then, explode the barrels.

But not before stealing all the gold that was reserved for the winners.

Blackstone hired a team of horses to pull the wagon. I had a healthy distrust of the animals. They whinnied and brayed incessantly. One of them tried to bite me when I came close.

"We're never going to get through the city unseen with these beasts," I muttered under my breath. "What was the point of waiting until night? Everybody within ten leagues is going to hear us!"

Blackstone chuckled. "Sometimes, the hardest things to see are those right under your nose." He unfurled a rolled up cloth and tacked it to the side of the wagon. It read, *The King's Brew*.

"That's never going to work," I said skeptically.

Blackstone grinned at me. "Want to bet?"

"No." I could tell he was feeling smug. "But if we get caught, I'm just a runaway who jumped on your wagon when you weren't looking. You don't know me."

"Fair enough." Blackstone's eyes glimmered. "And if we don't?"

"If we don't," I said, "I'll admit that you're a luck-struck bastard."

Blackstone threw his head back and laughed.

***

Later that hour, we were rolling down the middle of an abandoned city street. I was huddled in the back with the barrels of explosives. Blackstone was steering the wagon and singing at the top of his lungs:

The King's men said,

Give us a drink,

The old King said,

Not for your dink!

I cringed every time we passed a guard post.

But, to my surprise, nobody stopped us. The wagon bumped and rattled and jolted all the way to our destination. The movement was actually rhythmic enough that I could almost have fallen asleep, were it not for the off-key singing.

I shot up when we lurched to a stop. I heard Blackstone's voice, low and urgent. "Dagan. Get out here!"

I scrambled up and ducked out from under the canopy.

The street was dark. Old buildings leaned in around us. I wondered how long it would be until one of them fell.

Everything was quiet aside from a small whicker every once in a while from the horses.

Blackstone motioned me to his side. "Stay close," he said, "and keep quiet. If anybody asks, you're my apprentice."

I nodded.

Blackstone walked to a pair of low cellar doors leading to one of the larger buildings. They lay close to the ground, almost completely horizontal.

He knelt down and banged on them with his fist.

We waited. I heard footsteps from the other side, followed by the clatter of locks being opened. One of the doors lifted and a man peered out.

He had a gap between his front teeth and a head completely devoid of hair. His nose was twisted from one-too-many street fights. Patchy stubble lined his cheeks, and he smelled a little like cheese.

He glared at Blackstone. "Whaddaya want?"

"Greetings, friend," Blackstone said, putting on a country accent. "I've got a delivery of the finest King's Ale this side of the Sephinx for you. Six barrels of the stuff, freshly brewed and delicious."

"Do you, now?" The man eyed Blackstone. He looked past him at the wagon, ignoring me completely. "You got yer papers?"

"Sure do," Blackstone said cheerily. He pulled out a few loose sheets from his pocket and handed them to the man who took them and started to read. I noticed his eyes moving from right to left, instead of left to right.

I struggled to keep my face straight. Blackstone might as well have handed him a recipe for a roast turkey. The man was illiterate.

"Here." He handed the papers back to Blackstone with a grunt. He lifted the door he was holding up and stepped out. "C'mon. I'll show y'the way in."

As we trailed after him, Blackstone looked down at me and winked.

We walked to the other side of the building. Two large doors, each double the height of a man, loomed before us. Our guide unhooked a ring of keys from his side, flipped through them with his finger, picked one out, and stuck it into the lock.

The doors opened.

Inside was a long, paved path sloping down. I could not see far into the darkness.

"I'll get the torches lit," the man said. "You bring yer wagon 'round here, and we can roll the barrels down." He pointed. "That's where they go."

My heart froze in my chest at the mention of his help. If the man handled any of the barrels, he'd realize in a second that they weren't filled with liquid.

Blackstone stepped in quickly. "I don't want t'be troubling you, friend," he said in that fake accent. "You've already provided us with more than enough assistance." He took out a gold coin from his pouch and pressed it into the man's hand. "For your effort," he said, then gestured off-handedly to me. "I brought this scrappy fellow t'help."

The man looked at me and grunted. Then, he turned his attention to the coin in his hand. His eyes widened for a moment when he saw that it was real gold.

He covered it quickly. "Yeh, fine, that ain't a problem," he said, suddenly too-toady. He gave Blackstone an elaborate bow.

"Pleasure doin' business wit you, sir. Just knock on my door again when yer done and I'll come back 'ere and lock up."

Blackstone tipped his hat in reply.

As the man scrambled off, I tugged on Blackstone's sleeve. "Did you really mean to give him a *gold* mark?" I asked. "That's more than he makes in a month!"

Blackstone chuckled. "I doubt he'll protest. And if it gets him to leave us alone…?" He trailed off, leaving the rest unsaid.

I followed Blackstone to the wagon. He grabbed the horses' reins and tugged on them. The team followed us back, each step of their hooves making a distinctive *clop.*

We returned to the open doors. The inside of the building was still dark. Blackstone led the horses farther away, then came back and picked up the torch hanging on the door. He lit it carefully with a match from his pocket, then handed it to me.

"There are others every five paces," he explained. "Run down and get them lit. I'll keep an eye on our cargo."

I nodded and ventured inside.

I saw the brick ceiling as soon as enough of the side torches were burning. It curved in a concave arc above me. When I saw that, I understood that the outside of the building was simply a façade. Nobody actually lived here. There was no space. The outer walls of the building were a way to mask this tunnel.

As I made my way down, I was reminded uncomfortably of Three-Grin's dungeons. The tunnel didn't smell, praise Xune, but it still gave off similar vibes.

At the very bottom, I reached another set of locked doors. I heard somebody moving behind me, and looked over to find Blackstone's silhouette against the night sky. He was laboring with one of the barrels.

I ran to help. He set it down and tipped it onto its side. "Careful now," he said, shooting the torches a warning look.

My eyes darted to them. Knives and even magic were all fine. But black powder that burst into flames a thousand times more powerful than the spark that lit it? That made me uncomfortable.

We rolled the barrel down and righted it in the corner opposite the nearest torch. Then we came back up and proceeded with the rest.

In the end, we had all six standing side-by-side in one corner. Blackstone straightened and looked at the doors.

"They're locked," I pointed out.

"I can see that." He tugged on the lock and gave a grunt of displeasure. "A twelve-pin. Nearly impenetrable."

"You can open it, can't you?"

"Yes, but I need more light." He gestured vaguely around the room. "It'll take too long in the dark. If the man who let us in comes back, he'll wonder why we're still here. Usually the deliveries get left here." Blackstone tapped the nearest barrel. "They get picked up in the morning."

"So what?" I asked. "Is that it? Don't you have another plan?"

"I do," he said.

"What is it?"

"You."

CHAPTER TWENTY-SEVEN

I crept down the long, dark alley, angling my path toward the cellar doors where we had first been greeted.

Blackstone's plan was simple. Well, simple for him, anyway.

It involved me breaking into the building, sneaking up on the man undetected, and swiping that ring of keys from his belt.

As I said, simple for *him*.

The first order of business was finding an alternate way inside. I couldn't go through the cellar doors. That meant I had to find a window or back door or *something* that would let me in.

I circled the building once, searching. The closest I could find was a second story window left slightly ajar.

But it was too high for me to reach. The siding of the building was plain mortar. I could not climb it.

I was crouching in the shadows under an opposing eave, considering my options, when I heard the sound of another wagon approaching.

I ducked out of my hiding spot and looked to the road. I saw a large cart, with a canvas thrown over the back to hide whatever its cargo was. It was pulled by a team of two donkeys.

Immediately, the familiarity of that sight gripped me. I'd seen a cart like that before. I'd *been* on a cart like that before.

It was coming toward me. I slipped back into the shadows and waited for it to pass. I saw the driver as the cart came closer. I half-expected him to be the same white-haired man who was supposed to bring me to the Arena.

Of course, that was a silly boyhood fear. That man was dead. I had seen the arrow between his eyes.

The man driving this cart had a reputable air about him. As the cart passed, I heard a very human mewl come from the back.

I froze and strained my ears. The sound did not come again. But I was certain of what it was.

The driver stopped in front of the building I was surveilling. He pounded on the same doors that Blackstone had. After a minute, the bald man popped out.

"Delivery, courtesy of Three-Grin," the cart driver said. He hitched a thumb over his shoulder. "Fresh meat for the Arena."

The other man nodded. "Let's see."

I crept closer as they walked to the back of the cart.

The driver flipped the canvas up. The reek of shit and piss wafted over to me.

My stomach turned. I saw cages, stacked on top of each other. Every cage had a destitute-looking child inside.

The man receiving the cart brought a kerchief to his nose. "Stinky little bastards," he cursed. He motioned for the driver to lower the canvas. "All right, all right. Come on. You know where they go."

The driver clicked his tongue and pulled on the reins. The donkeys stepped after him. They went in the opposite direction of where Blackstone was waiting.

Before they left, the bald man turned and lowered the door to the cellar. He did not lock it.

I recognized my chance to get into the building. But I hesitated. If I followed the man, I had a shot at stealing the keys from him. If I went inside, perhaps I could find another way to Blackstone and open the doors from within.

In the end, I decided to go in. The man with the keys would return at some point. Even if I didn't find a path to Blackstone, I could still wait for him and get the keys then.

I looked both ways to ensure the street was empty, and ran across. I lifted one heavy cellar door and dropped inside.

I discovered a long set of stairs in the darkness. I had to trail one hand along the wall for guidance.

When I reached the bottom, I could see a flickering light come from beneath the door of one far room. I started toward it.

I passed a few rooms on my way, all unoccupied and dark. I pressed my ear to the door with the light and held my breath for a count of ten. When I didn't hear anything, I slipped in.

The room was plainly furnished. An open bottle of wine sat atop a table in the middle of the room. A bed stood to one side. There were some shelves with random, useless things on them. It was the type of room you might expect to find in an inn.

Something did not feel right.

Blackstone taught me how deceiving appearances could be. He taught me that the best secrets are those that can be hidden in plain sight.

This room was as plain as they go. So, I began to search for its secret.

Call it a hunch or a guess. Call it some type of intuition. I knew, somewhere deep down, that this room was more than it appeared.

I started with the walls. I ran my fingers along each of them, searching for a groove that might reveal a secret entrance. I found none.

I worked on the shelves, thinking there might be a mechanism that opens some compartment. I did not find any.

I looked behind the shelving. *Nothing*.

Frustrated, I leaned against one corner of the bed. That's when I heard voices coming from down the hall.

I ran to the door. The voices were getting closer. Too close for me to sneak out.

I spun back and looked frantically around the room. There was nowhere to go. I was caught.

My heart started pounding hard in my chest. I would be discovered.

Faced with no other options, I did the only thing a boy of ten could.

I dropped down and rolled under the bed.

No sooner did my body disappear than the door burst open. I saw two pairs of feet. I crept slightly closer to the edge to peer out.

The two men I saw conversing outside were now here.

"…some bloke brought in a whole wagonload of King's Ale," the bald man confided. "Now, I dun remember ever orderin' none such. But, I'm not a man to deny a little free drink if the occasion serves, eh?" He elbowed his friend in the ribs. "I had him bring it down t'where all the deliveries go. If a few of those barrels end up missing by mornin'…" He chuckled. "…I dun think anyone'll be the wiser."

"You ratty son of a bitch," the driver grinned.

The other man laughed. "I know, I know. It's a perk o' the job." He knelt down and pulled away a rug that covered a large space in the middle of the room.

There was a crawlspace door under it.

I hit my forehead against my arm. *Idiot*! I thought. Of course the secret entrance would be in the most obvious place.

The man lifted the latch and picked up a lantern. He lit it with a long match, snuffed the flame between his fingers, and held the lantern out in front of him as he descended the steps.

"Come on," he said. "We've got hours yet 'till the morn. I say, it's time for us t'get roaring drunk!"

The cart driver laughed and followed the other man down.

I waited until their voices faded before rolling out of my spot and following them. My steps were soft and my movement light. As soon as I hit the bottom of the stairs, I saw the glow of the lantern in the distance.

I followed it.

The men were going to open the very doors Blackstone was waiting at. That was a problem. One, because they would be suspicious when they found him still there. Two, because the moment they opened the barrels, they would discover them full of black powder, not ale.

My feet were silent against the hard floor. The two men turned through a doorway at the end of the hall. I ran through without pause. I was so focused on the lantern flame that I did not notice the black shapes lurking by the doorway.

Two arms wrapped around me and lifted me off my feet. I was too surprised to react.

"Gotcha, ya little bastard," the bald man hissed in my ear. He threw me to the ground. I landed with a grunt and spun around.

Two shapes were present in the darkness: the bald man, and the driver beside him. My eyes darted to the lantern that I thought was still moving. It was not. It hung from a side hook in the distance.

"Now, y'v got ten words t'explain what the 'ell you've bin doin' followin' us," the bald man growled. I saw the shine of steel being drawn. "Or else I gut yeh like a pig."

I looked from him to the driver. Both were large men—at least, they seemed large to a boy of my size. The dancing light from the lantern cast menacing shadows on their faces. It made them look more fearsome than they probably were.

"Well?" he demanded. "Speak up, boy!" He stepped closer.

I knew I only had one chance. And for it to work, I had to move fast.

Instinct kicked in. I sprang to my feet. Two knives appeared in my hands. Before either man could react, I flung one at each of their throats.

The first knife sunk right into the bald man's Adam's apple. A look of disbelief flashed on his face. He went down with a wet, gurgling sound, choking on his own blood.

But my other throw was off. In the dark, it was difficult to judge distance and space.

I hit the cart driver in the shoulder.

Rage erupted across his features. He drew his short sword and lunged for me.

I leapt back, avoiding the killing blow aimed for my chest by a hair. The man grunted and swung again. His blade arced down in a violent swing.

I rolled to my left. The sword rang off the stony ground. Adrenaline rushed through my body and blood thundered in my ears. I had no time to contemplate my next move as the man thrust again.

I found my ivory knife in my hands. I parried the blow. The shock of it sent a tremor through my arm.

A vicious grin spread across the driver's face when he saw the weapon I was defending myself with. The odds were clearly in his favor. I was weak. He was strong. I was little. He was big. It was not a fair fight, and both of us knew it.

When he lunged again, I waited for the last moment to jump back from the blow, at the same time parrying it with my small blade. The force ripped the knife from my hand, and I cried out.

I also misjudged where I was. My feet landed in a slick puddle of blood and slid out from under me. My ankle twisted, and I fell.

The cart driver blinked in momentary surprise. Then, he straightened. He walked toward me slowly, savoring his assured victory.

I scrambled back. Hot blood surrounded me. The thick liquid coated my hands and legs and back. I grabbed for one of my throwing knives. To my horror, I found it stuck in the sheath. My wet fingers could not get a good enough grip to pull it out.

"Tell me," he said, "how a little, useless rat like you manages to kill a grown man?" He gestured at the body on the ground. "A lucky throw? A stroke of fate?" He reached up and ripped my knife out of his shoulder, then threw it to the ground.

It rattled and bounced before coming to a stop.

"Well, boy," the man said, "it doesn't matter now, anyway. Your luck's run out."

He thrust his sword down. I closed my eyes and thought I was going to die.

But instead of piercing through my chest, ,the sword sunk deep into my upper leg. My eyes burst open and I screamed.

The driver knelt beside me. He twisted his weapon. Excruciating pain ripped through me. "But now is not your time to die, boy. I'm going to make you fodder for the Arena. Tomorrow night, with thousands of people screaming for your blood, you will know what true terror is."

He sneered at me and brought his face inches from mine. His putrid breath fell on my skin as he spoke. "Tomorrow," he twisted his sword again, "you will die when—"

He did not get to finish his sentence. His eyes widened, and he looked down at his chest, where my last throwing knife had sunk into his heart.

He gave a dying sputter, spat a mouthful of blood at me, then fell to the side.

I sagged back as my fingers unclenched the knife. I had been able to free it at the last moment.

I was breathing hard. My entire body felt like it was on fire. My hair was matted with blood, and my clothes were completely drenched.

Only by the greatest effort of will did I manage to push myself to a sitting position. I looked at the sword sticking through my leg. Blood bubbled out from where the metal bit into my skin.

My hands shook as I brought them to the hilt. My breathes started coming faster and faster in anticipation. I closed my eyes, counted to three, and pulled *up*.

The pain that tore through me was worse than when the man had stabbed my leg. My eyes burst open and I emitted the most soul-wrenching, heart-rending cry imaginable.

Blood gushed out of the wound like water from a geyser. I could feel my leg burning. As quickly as I could, I cut a long strap from one of the dead men's coats and wrapped it around the gash. I gritted my teeth and winced against the pain, but I did not scream again.

Call it a re-awakening of a talent I had forgotten I had. I hadn't experienced pain of the sort my leg felt since my time with Three-Grin. Back then, my body and mind had learned to work in harmony to shelter me from the agony that defined my everyday existence. That ability had been lost somewhere during my time with Alicia. But it returned to me now with a hungry vengeance.

I allowed my mind to collect the pain and bundle it into a small ball to hide somewhere far away. As I tied the final knot around my leg, I was barely even conscious of the wound.

I picked myself up, and hobbled over to where the bald man lay. My movements were uneven and lurching. Just because I could will the pain away did not mean my body could somehow overcome the very real disability of a gaping hole in its thigh.

I found the ring of keys on the man's belt and took it. I stumbled toward one wall, and, using my arm for support, began the long, heavy walk to where Blackstone was waiting.

I cannot remember a speck of that journey. All I know is that somehow, I managed to carry the lantern, the keys, and my ivory knife all the way to those two guard doors and open them from within. I do not even know how I found them, given my half-lucid state, especially since I had no visualization of the building's floorplan in my mind.

Blackstone rushed to me as soon as the doors opened. I must have made a horrifying sight, covered as I was in blood.

"By the gods," he muttered, "what happened to you, Dagan?"

"Fight," I managed, before falling into his arms and passing out.

Chapter Twenty-Eight

When I came to, the first thought that rushed through my head was that we were too late.

The Arena's main event was supposed to be the following night. I was dead-certain that I'd been out for days. We'd missed our chance to kill Three-Grin, destroy the Arena, and pull off the caper of a lifetime.

But as I blinked away the haziness in my vision, and the feel of my body returned to me, I realized that I was lying on the ground outside the two massive doors. We were still underground. I rolled my head to one side, looking up to the entrance of the tunnel. It was still night.

A harsh, jerking motion at my leg yanked my attention down.

Blackstone was kneeling over me, tightening a belt around the flesh wound. He was chewing on some sort of leaf. I watched as he spat it out and rubbed it into my leg.

I steeled myself for another shot of searing pain. None came. It wasn't because I had buried the pain away, either. I relaxed my mind, letting go of that tight ball…

A numbness encompassed my entire leg.

"You're up," Blackstone grunted. He did not sound happy. "Dammit, kid, what the hell got into you? I saw what you did to those two men. We were supposed to do this *without* attracting attention!"

"They… jumped me," I said. My head felt woozy, probably from the loss of blood.

Blackstone made a sound of displeasure. "You got caught?"

"I—"

"You *slipped*," he corrected. He yanked the belt around my leg tighter. I felt the slightest bit of pressure.

Then again, it could have been my imagination. The leg was as leaden as a log.

"What did you do?" I asked, looking down at the wound.

"*Laciruss*," Blackstone grumbled. "It's a plant that takes away the pain. Dulls your senses."

I could tell by his tone there was something he was omitting. "But?" I asked.

"But," Blackstone sat back and exhaled, "unless you wash it out of your system in time, you risk the effects becoming permanent. It'll kill all the nerves in your leg."

"How long do we have?" I asked.

"Twelve hours. Maybe more, if you're lucky. But I wouldn't take the chance, if I were you."

"The fight's not until later tonight," I said. "We can still make it!"

Blackstone extended his hand to me. I took it.

"Come on," he said, pulling me up. "If we get back to my home, I know an apothecary that carries the antidote. We'll get it to you in time."

I stared at him. "You mean we're going to *leave*?"

Blackstone grimaced. "The Arena is just one job, Dagan. Your leg—you'll have to live with that forever."

"But Three-Grin is going to be here!" I cried. "I thought this was our chance to kill him? You told me he doesn't come to watch the fights!"

"Aye, and so we'll miss him," Blackstone said. "But the price isn't worth it. You're wounded. You won't be able to do your part."

I staggered away from him, supporting myself. "I will!" I proclaimed. My numb leg felt like it would give out on me at any moment. I fought to keep it straight. "No. No! We can't give up now. No. We won't!"

"Dagan." Blackstone laid a hand on my shoulder. "Trust me. I have been looking forward to this day as much as you. But losing the feeling in your leg permanently? That would be as good as crippling you. It's not worth it."

"We have time," I protested. "If we rush—"

"No." Blackstone shook his head. "You cannot run. You can barely walk. Both of us need to be able-bodied to pull this off."

"I got back to you," I said. "I did it without any *Laciruss* in my system."

"You were running on adrenaline."

"I was still *running*!" I said. "We can do it. We'll get the antidote. Come back. I'll have the feeling in my leg, and—"

Blackstone cut me off. "I admire your courage, son. I really do. But the minute you drink the antidote, the pain will consume you. You'll be even worse off than you are now."

"I can handle it," I promised. "I swear. We need to do this. We have to, Black!"

Blackstone peered deep into my eyes. I felt the intensity radiate out from him.

I matched it one-to-one.

"We *have* to," I said again. "Please?"

He continued to stare at me. Finally, he spoke.

"This is your heart talking? You are not blinded by your desire for revenge?"

"No!" I said. "I'm not—well, I *am*, I *do* want revenge. But it's not what's driving me. You taught me to push it down. I know what we have to do. I'm still up for it!"

Blackstone stood up. He walked a few paces away. "Walk to me," he said.

I gritted my teeth and began to march. Every second step sent me lurching to one side. My leg felt as if it were filled with liquid metal.

"You cannot balance," Blackstone observed. "You would be useless in a fight. The muscle in your leg is severed." He shook his head. "You won't be able to walk once the *Laciruss* is gone."

"I will," I insisted. "I can do it!" I could feel hot tears welling up in my eyes. "We're so *close*!"

"Dagan, I've seen men twice your size take wounds half as big and be dragged screaming off the battlefield. You're young, and fueled by courage. But this is not something we can pull off any longer."

"So that's it?" I spat. "You're just going to abandon it, because of me?"

"There will be other jobs."

"But none as important as this one! Please. I saw another cart filled with children delivered tonight. They were in cages, Black. They are all going to die if we don't do something!"

Blackstone's face darkened. "You saw a cart?" he said.

"Yes!" I exclaimed. "The man I killed drove it here. He said it was from Three-Grin."

Something changed in Blackstone's expression. His face turned hard.

"I rode to Hallengard in a cage," he said under his breath. "That day, I vowed I would destroy the Arena and all those like Three-Grin." He looked at me. "You truly believe you're up to task?"

Hope bloomed in my chest. "Yes!" I exclaimed.

Blackstone looked at me. I could feel his eyes weighing. Judging.

I stood as tall as I could. I was not about to back down now.

"All right," he nodded. "We will try. But we have to hurry."

CHAPTER TWENTY-NINE

The Arena was past the massive doors and down another long, sloping tunnel. When we came to it, I was astounded by its sheer *size*.

It looked like a crater dug underground. It was a circular space surrounded by rows upon rows of old, wooden benches. I stared in wonder at how many people must be able to fit in those seats. Thousands. *Tens* of thousands.

Blackstone led our team of horses around while I sat in the back of the wagon. I hated feeling so useless, but riding was much faster for me than walking.

The barrels surrounded me. We took a path that wound below the structure of the Arena. Blackstone said he knew about it from his time here. It was a maintenance path, running underneath the enormous structure. Down there, I could see all the planks of wood that made up the Arena's base.

He knew the six spots where he wanted to plant the explosives. We rode around, circling the outer rim. Once every forty planks, Blackstone would stop and deposit a barrel against a massive vertical pillar. He bound it tight with a heavy rope, and we continued on.

In time, all six barrels were in position. By some stroke of luck, we did not come across another person during our entire escapade. Blackstone had me keep watch, armed with a new set of throwing knives. He told me to kill on sight.

I suspected it was just his way of making me feel useful. He undoubtedly planned the route beforehand so that we wouldn't encounter anyone.

At some point, I heard whimpering below us. I looked at the ledge where the floor met the wall, and saw small air ducts leaving little gaps in the wood.

"The slavers keep the children even deeper," Blackstone said when he noticed me looking. "They're left in separate pens before the fights. I lived it."

A shiver ran down my spine. If not for that miraculous rescue, I would have died down there long ago.

An uncomfortable thought occurred to me. "Tonight," I said, "if all goes according to plan… what happens to the fighters?"

Blackstone did not look at me when he answered. "They will burn."

I sputtered. "*What*?"

"We cannot save the ones already taken. Their fate has been decided. All we can do is save others from a similar existence."

I stared at him in disbelief.

He sighed. "I know what you're thinking. But even if we could save them, Dagan—and we cannot—where would they go? What would happen to them after? They would die on the streets. They are nearly feral. Their humanity has been stripped from them. They will not survive."

"They will have a chance!" I said. I remembered the scared little boy I had woken up next to in the cart. "By leaving them, you condemn them to death!"

"Such is the way of the world. They would have died without us. What difference does it make if they die because of us?"

"It makes a difference," I stated. I could not verbalize *how*, but I knew it did.

"There is nothing more we can do." Something about Blackstone's tone told me the conversation was over.

I brooded in silence as Blackstone turned the wagon back up. I was dimly aware of my leg. I was more worried about the fighters.

Blackstone said we couldn't save them. I didn't doubt that was the truth. But I still thought that we should at least *try*.

On our way up, Blackstone stopped by the two bodies I had left. He cleaned up some of the blood and arranged them in a position to make it look like their death was the result of a brawl gone bad.

"Not the most elegant solution," he said, "but it'll have to do."

I grunted my agreement. I was still bitter about leaving the slaves.

You see, back then, I had childish notions of honor and justice in my mind. I had seen little of the world. My moral compass had not yet been corrupted by the bitter truths of life.

Here are those truths as I know them now:

Life is hard. Life is unfair. There is no such thing as justice. To chase after it in the vain hope of attaining some metaphysical glory or feeling of self-righteousness is a fool's errand. Things will always be bleak and cold in this world. Do not try to change that. It would be as fruitless as trying to change when the sun rises.

The weak do not survive. The strong always win. Some of those caught in the middle plod along, living off whatever scraps they might find. But it is a thin existence. When you are young you believe you can change that.

You cannot.

I have told you once before that my story will teach you the folly of being a hero. That was my life for many years. I know better, now, just the same as Blackstone knew back then.

He was a good teacher. Do not fault him for not instilling the merciless nature of the world into me at the time. He knew I would have to make my own mistakes to learn.

The first mistake I made came later that night. It cost me dearly.

CHAPTER THIRTY

We'd gotten back to Blackstone's home, and he brought me the antidote. It was a dark blue liquid in a tiny vial half the width of my pinkie.

On his request, I waited until after he'd stitched up the wound before taking it. I'd also changed out of my blood-soaked clothes.

I swallowed the potion. Blackstone told me to lie down in anticipation of the pain. To show him I was strong, I remained standing.

I waited for a few minutes. Nothing happened. I was about to suggest that maybe he'd gotten the wrong vial, when an avalanche of pain and agony crashed into me.

I staggered to the wall. The world turned white. My entire leg felt like it was on fire. No. It was more than that. It was the feeling you might experience if you were dipped into a pot of boiling water. The pain was not just isolated to my leg. It consumed my entire body.

Using every ounce of strength I had, I collected that pain and pushed it into the deepest corner of my mind. I fought as it throbbed and tried to break free. It wanted to overwhelm me.

I gritted my teeth and willed it down.

My vision returned. The sequence felt like it had lasted seconds, but when I returned to myself, I felt my shirt drenched in sweat. It must have been minutes.

I pushed off the wall. The pain wasn't entirely gone—I could still feel a dull throb in my leg—but I had to leave that if I wanted to retain any control over the limb.

I walked toward Blackstone, who was watching me with dark, hooded eyes. My first few steps were uneven, but as I got closer, they levelled out.

"Where did you learn to do that?" he asked. His voice was grave.

I looked at him. "What?"

"The Flame of Souls. It is a powerful mental trick. Who taught you?"

I looked at him without comprehension. "Nobody taught me."

"It takes many years of practice to achieve what you just did, Dagan. I have not told you about it. I will repeat myself only once. Who. Taught. You?"

I shook my head. "Nobody taught me. It's just something I… knew."

His eyes focused on me. "Since when? For how long? Why have you not used it before?"

"In Three-Grin's dungeons," I said. I thought of Alicia. "Before I could speak. I didn't know it was something special. It was just something I did."

"And since then?" Blackstone grilled. "Have you used it since?"

"No," I said. "It was just a way of dealing with pain. I haven't had to. I don't even think I could, before I got stabbed today."

"Come here, Dagan." Blackstone motioned me closer. "Sit down. Let me tell you something."

I climbed up next to him.

"The Flame of Souls is not just a *way of dealing with pain*. It is so much more than that. It is a way of controlling your sleeping mind. It takes years—decades—of practice to achieve what you just did.

"It is a remarkable talent. It allows you to unlock the full potential of what's in here." He tapped the side of his head. "Most people aren't even aware they *have* a sleeping mind. But it's the most important part of you. It houses your instincts. It gives birth to your feelings. It controls the thousands of different processes that keep you alive. The ones you don't think about, like breathing. It works in the background to form new ideas and solve problems. It is most active when you sleep.

"You know the saying, 'sleep on it'? It has a double meaning. When you close your eyes to rest, your conscious mind is suppressed. It takes a step back and allows the sleeping mind to come forward. That is why you dream. That is why *sleep* is so important. It seals new memories. It strengthens old ones. It helps you learn the things you practiced that day.

"When you sleep on a problem, you allow that part of you to function unabated. The sleeping mind does not compete. It churns away in the background, and floats to the surface only when you rest.

"Everyone's mind is capable of astounding feats. Most of those—intuition, common sense, problem solving, self-discovery—come from the sleeping mind. It is also where your reservoir of magic exists."

Blackstone exhaled. "If magic still remained in our world in full force, I believe you would have had the potential to become the greatest sorcerer of our time. If you stumbled upon the Flame of Souls by yourself, when you were no more than a babe... well, it's fascinating to think of the things you could have achieved if you were born in a different age."

He glanced at me. "Don't let that go to your head. The Flame of Souls is an impressive achievement. But it is also dangerous. It grants you access to the parts of your mind that are usually locked off. Things like breathing. Your heartbeat. Pain tolerance.

"I am warning you of the dangers now, Dagan. Do you remember the rings I drew once? I would have spoken to you about the Flame only after you have reached the fifth level. Even then, it would have likely been too early. But I know that you already show great promise.

"If you have control over such functions of your body, you can easily abuse them. Do you want to feign death? Enter the Flame of Souls and stop your heart while an enemy checks your pulse. Want to hold your breath under water? Enter the Flame of Souls and delay your need to breathe.

"But it is only a mental thing, Dagan. Your brain still needs blood. Your lungs still need air. Through the Flame of Souls, you control the *process* of achieving those things, but you cannot change your *physical need* for them.

"Do you understand what I'm saying? You must be very careful. The Flame of Souls allows you unparalleled control over your body. You can dull the senses in your arm and dip it into boiling oil. Will you feel pain? No. Will you hand be ruined? *Yes.*"

I understood the dangers. They were the same ones I suspected when Blackstone started to speak. "Are you saying I shouldn't use it, then?" I asked. "Ever?"

Blackstone shook his head. "No. It is a gift. To deny it would be madness. Just be aware that while the Flame of Souls might make you feel invincible, you are still as human as the rest of us."

"I will," I nodded.

"Good," Blackstone replied. He flashed a grin. "But with this new revelation, I am confident that we can achieve everything we want tonight."

Chapter Thirty-One

Blackstone told me the rest of the plan on our way there.

The Arena was divided into three levels. The spectator suites were on the upper ring. The richest and most revered patrons had the privilege of watching from there. Three-Grin, along with the other slavers, would be the guests of honor tonight.

The second level was comprised of all the benches I had seen circling the fighting ground. There, some twenty-odd-thousand people would sit and cheer.

The third and final level made up the pens where the fighters were kept. Blackstone and I had planted explosives there earlier.

Hours before the fight, bets would start to pour in. The odds of each fighter were posted on a board outside. It was organized by the less-than-reputable bankers of the city.

You would think that an event of this size would draw the attention of Hallengard's rulers at some point. You'd be right. It had. However, the organizers of the Arena had established a kind of uneasy allegiance with the ruling class that let the Arena function.

The fights satisfied the people's thirst for blood. They prevented the lower and middle class from growing bored and stirring up real trouble. The children who served as fighters were nobodies. They had no homes, no families, no mothers or fathers to care for them. They were raised only to fight.

In return for turning a blind eye, the city's rulers received very generous donations after each fight—sometimes, as much as half of total earnings. Enough money poured in for the organizers to afford such a hefty tax.

The bets closed half an hour before the first fight. All the money collected would be transported to a secure storage room on the highest level. It would be tallied, and a portion of it would be divvied up in anticipation of the night's winners. The rest of it filled the pockets of all those involved in the fighting ring.

Blackstone had his sights on that storage room.

The plan was simple: Start a fire in the upper levels that would spread through the rest of the Arena. Break into the storage room in the ensuing commotion. Get out before the barrels beneath the Arena blew.

I would serve as a decoy. The slavers were allowed a special place, separate from the rest of the crowd. Anybody could claim to be a slaver if they provided a child as sacrifice. Three-Grin and the other three simply had a special position because they were the best.

Blackstone would enter me into the fights. I was a little old, but he said if I acted meek and kept my head down, we shouldn't have any trouble overcoming that. It would grant him access to the slaver's spectator platform. He would sneak to the highest level from there.

My job was to light the barrels we'd planted at the proper time. The fire Blackstone would start should reach the lower levels and cause the barrels to blow eventually, but we didn't want to leave that to chance.

Blackstone outfitted a crude rope around my neck to serve as a leash. He held the other end. That is how we made our way through the streets that night.

As we got closer to the Hells, the crowds thickened. Anybody could tell there was something special going on tonight.

We passed the building where I saw the cart deliver the children, then turned down a side alley. I looked over my shoulder and saw the stream of people passing the entrance on the main street. The crowd was loud and lively. The smell of alcohol permeated the air.

"Remember," Blackstone reminded me under his breath, "you're deaf, mute, and dumb."

I nodded in reply, starting the act early.

"And keep your head down like I said."

I lowered my eyes until I could see nothing but the dirt on my boots.

Blackstone banged his fist against a decrepit wooden door. After a few seconds, a sliding eyehole came open. A man regarded us from inside.

"What do you want?" he asked in a strangely squeaky voice.

Blackstone tugged on my leash, and I stumbled forward. "This pissling's been nothin' but trouble for me," he said, in another of his peasant accents. "He's lazy. He don't work. He can't speak, and he's dumb as rocks." Blackstone hit me upside the head to demonstrate. I feigned a whimper. "Meek, too. Won't life a finger against a soul."

The man behind the door chuckled. "And you want me to take him off your hands. That what you're saying?"

"He's not the best fighter," Blackstone conceded, "but he can be one of the early sacrifices t'get the crowd goin'. What d'ya say?"

"Let me take a look at him," the man answered. The viewer slid closed. I heard a scraping sound from inside. After a few seconds, the door opened.

The man who emerged stood halfway to Blackstone's chest.

He was an imp. I had to smooth my features forcibly lest I be caught staring. I'd never seen a little person before.

He waddled up to me and took my chin in his hand. I shied away, remembering Blackstone's reminder about *meekness*. His grip tightened, and he forced my eyes to his.

I tried to look frightened.

"How old is he?" the imp ask.

"Don't know," Blackstone said. "I found 'im when he was halfway grown, and had 'im for three years."

"Hmph." The imp stuck his finger in my mouth. He peered at my teeth.

"Still got some of his baby molars," he said.

"I reckon he'd be about seven, maybe eight," Blackstone pointed out.

"Nah." The imp shook his head. "Look at his face. His features are maturing." He took hold of my chin again and turned it toward Blackstone. "He's got to be at least ten. Maybe as old as twelve."

My heart sank in my chest. If I was too old, they wouldn't allow me in.

"I don't expect a premium for 'im," Blackstone said. "Jus' a few dimes would be enough."

The imp barked a laugh. "You want *dimes* for this runt? He better shit gold to be worth that much."

Blackstone tugged on the leash and yanked me toward him. "Too bad. I'd heard the Arena was lookin' for extra fighters tonight."

He pulled me after him as he started to walk away. "I can still sell him as a galley slave and get more than that," he muttered under his breath.

"Wait, wait, hold on, get back here," the imp said. "I didn't say I don't want him. Just that your price is too high."

Blackstone crossed his arms. "And what would you offer?"

"One dime," the imp said.

Blackstone turned and began down the alley.

"Okay, okay, wait! I'll give you two," the imp corrected. "Two dimes for the brat. You've got the look of an educated man about you. Y'know the kid's over age. I'll give you two dimes, and no more."

"Two and a third," Blackstone said.

The imp grumbled. "Two dimes and a silver penny. I won't go higher than that."

Blackstone stuck his hand out. "My friend," he said, "you've got yourself a deal."

***

The imp yanked on my leash and I stumbled and fell. He turned around to kick at me.

"Get up, you useless sack of rotting bones," he cursed. He tugged the leash. "I said, get up!"

I staggered to my feet, doing my best to appear beaten. We were in a narrow corridor a few levels beneath the earth. Torches along the walls provided light.

"Good," he said. He turned away and continued on, pulling me after him.

He was shorter than me, fat, and stubby. My finger felt the hilts of the knives hidden in my clothes. I could kill him before he even turned around.

Instead, I kept my head down and trailed after him.

He led me through a series of doors, all of which were unlocked. The final one brought us to a dark, horrific place.

There were cages all around us. Each one had a child inside. Some bawled, some stared, and others appeared to be already dead.

The stink of human decay clung heavy to the air. The cages were stacked upon each other three-high.

The imp led me to an unoccupied one at the end of the room. He kicked the door open and shoved me in. I fell. My hands and knees splashed in urine.

He knelt down to work on the lock. Every once in a while the ceiling shook as a distant cheer sounded in the air.

"You hear that?" The imp grinned. "That's the crowd calling for your blood. I wouldn't get too comfortable. It'll be your turn up there, soon."

He didn't know I had no intention of dying that night.

He clamped the lock shut and walked away. I waited until he was out of the room to reach for my knives.

I sawed through the rope snug around my throat. When it fell, I felt like I could take my first deep breath in hours. So, I did.

That was a mistake. The putrid stench around me filled my nostrils and burned my tongue. I gagged and almost retched.

Steadying myself against the bars, I waited a few seconds to get used to the smells. Then, I turned around and extracted the long metal wire that was embedded inside the rope. There was not much light in the room, but even so, it didn't take me longer than a minute to pick the lock and free myself.

Blackstone had taught me well.

Next, I waited. The fighters for the first round had already been selected. There would be six matches before the intermission. That break would give Blackstone the opportunity to sneak up to the highest levels. It would also be when the imp returned to wheel out the next group. They would go right before the championship fight—the one Three-Grin was here to watch.

As I waited, I tried not to see all the human faces around me. Blackstone told me the slaves could not be saved. Leaving them to their fate dug at me. I tried to push those feelings down, the same way I kept the pain in my leg at bay. But, I couldn't. Not fully. Getting rid of the sense of injustice was, for some reason, a lot harder than ignoring the screaming agony of my wound.

When the cheers stopped coming, I knew the intermission had begun. I scrambled out of the cage and ducked behind it, hiding in the shadows.

The imp returned minutes later. I cursed when I saw he wasn't alone. Two large, bulky men with skin the color of *kaf* trailed him. They had a trolley between them with wheels on the bottom.

The imp went around the room, pointing out different cages. "This one, this one, and this one," he said, jabbing a fat finger out each time. The two men picked those cages up and deposited them onto the cart.

I tensed as they neared mine. The imp hadn't noticed I was gone. "This one, this one, that one," he continued. The two men ran to do his bidding.

I gripped the hilts of my knives tightly. I judged the newcomers to be the greater threats. I edged sideways, positioning myself so I was right in front of them...

"HEY!" the imp cried out. "Hey, this cage's empty!"

That was my cue. One knife flew from my hand. It flashed through the air and found one of the big man's throats. He fell to the ground, dead.

His friend snarled and whipped around. "There!" he cried, pointing at me. I did not have the right angle to throw at him, so I shoved my shoulder in the stack of cages separating us and pushed. They toppled forward and crashed to the ground.

I heard moans erupt from the children around me, but no cries. I didn't have time to consider the significance of that as I leapt out and threw my next knife.

The large man was moving toward me. He saw the blade in the air, and twisted sideways just in time to avoid it. It skimmed his arm and lodged itself into the wooden bars of another cage.

But I was prepared for that. No sooner had the first knives left my hands than two more were there. I rolled to the side as the large man smashed through the cages to try to get to me, and threw.

One knife landed in his ribs. He roared, but the sound only lasted the half-second it took for the next one to sink into his throat.

His hands clutched at his neck. But, he was already forgotten to me. I leapt over the upturned cages, my eyes focusing on the imp.

He had a cudgel in one hand. It wouldn't do much good against an enemy with a real weapon, but as it were, I was unarmed. Blackstone had only managed to hide four throwing knives on me before we left.

I landed on the floor next to the first body. My wounded leg gave out. Pain tore at the surface of that faraway knot, trying to break free. I fell. The imp saw his chance and rushed me.

He did not get far. I'd aimed my jump so that if I fell, I'd be within arm's reach of the first blade. I pulled it out of the dead man's throat and threw.

It spun over itself in the air before stopping with a dull *thud* right between the imp's eyes. The short man crumpled down, dead on the spot.

I sagged back. My heart thundered in my chest and I was panting. Forcibly, I slowed my breathing and my heartbeat. I was just about to get up when a crash from the side made my head whip around.

The man I thought I'd killed—the one with the knives in his side and throat—apparently wasn't ready to die just yet. He roared to his feet as blood streamed down his chest from the neck wound, and charged me.

I scrambled up in the nick of time and jumped out of the way. The man had found a long, metal pipe from somewhere. He lumbered toward me and swung.

I ducked to avoid the blow and felt the pipe swish right above my head. The man staggered with the momentum of the swing. I turned around and ran, as fast as my bad leg would carry me, toward the imp.

I slid to a stop beside him. I reached down and grabbed the hilt of the blade embedded in his skull. I pulled—and jerked the imp's whole body up with the force.

My knife was stuck.

I looked up just in time to see the man who should be dead aim another swing at my head. I ducked, but this time, I was too slow.

The pipe rebounded off the side of my head. The impact threw me to the ground. White stars exploded in my vision.

I blinked through the pain and forced it to join the dark ball at the back of my mind. I looked up, and saw the man standing over me.

I saw the blood coming from his throat. I saw the knife still impaled in his ribs. By all reason and logic, he should be long dead.

But, he wasn't. He stared at me like one of the Nehym. A thick vein pulsed up the side of his neck and over his forehead. He raised the pipe, steadying himself for the killing blow...

And grunted in surprise. He coughed. Blood splattered from his mouth.

Like an axed tree, he tipped over and fell to the side.

I stared in amazement, not knowing what the hell just happened. Then I picked out the small shape standing over the man's body.

It was one of the children from the cages. Somehow, he'd broken free. I saw my knife in his hand—the one that had lodged into a large bar. The blade was soaked red from where he'd just stabbed my assailant.

I pushed myself up, grunting as my bad leg almost caved again. "Thank you," I said.

The child looking at me opened his mouth. No sound came other than a low moan.

I saw past his teeth, and realized in horror that his tongue had been cut.

Suddenly, all the pathetic noises of the children around me made sense. They'd *all* had their tongues cut. That is why they did not shout or cry.

The roar of the crowd came from above me, shaking the dark room. The intermission was over. The next fights were about to begin.

The boy extended my knife to me.

"No," I said, shaking my head. "Keep it." I knew he couldn't understand me, so I took his hand and wrapped his fingers around the hilt. "For you," I said.

His lips moved as he tried to mimic the words.

Another roar rose from up high. It was time to go. But no matter what Blackstone said, I could not just leave these children to their fates. Not after one of them had saved me. I saw my face reflected in each of theirs. I saw the hope in the feral boy's eyes.

I would not leave them to burn.

"Here," I said, motioning to the boy. "Follow me. Hurry!"

I ran to the nearest cage and took the knife from him. I jammed it into the cheap lock and used a bit of leverage to break it open.

I pressed the knife back into his hand. "Go," I said, swinging my hand at the other cages. "Go. Free them!"

The boy understood. He took my knife and ran, kneeling beside the next cage to break the lock.

I rushed to gather my knives, wiped them clean, and stowed them back in their place. Then, I ran across the other side of the room, breaking the locks as quickly as I could.

A loud gong sounded above me. It signaled the end of the first fight. Five more, and then the signature one would begin.

I was already out of time. Blackstone would be expecting me to have lit the fuses by now.

My knife jammed in the lock. I jerked it, and the blade snapped from the force. I cursed. I saw the wide, hopeful eyes of the child inside fill with dread.

The gong sounded again. I whirled my head up. I had to go.

"I'm sorry," I said. The child in the cage looked at me without comprehension. "It's too late. I'm sorry."

I got up and ran.

I ran through the doors that led out of there. My leg slowed me. I was already late. I rushed through the corridors that led to the maintenance path below the Arena. I saw one guard slumbering by the door. I threw my knife without thinking, and retrieved it from his body as I passed, not slowing a step.

I skidded to a stop before the first barrel and reached for the little box of matches I'd hidden in one of my knife sheaths.

It was missing.

Alarm filled me. I spun back, looking at the ground, hoping I'd dropped it close by.

No such luck.

My hands patted down every pocket and secret compartment in my clothes. All were empty. The matches were not there.

The gong sounded a third time. The final fight would begin soon. That would be Blackstone's cue to spark the fire.

I looked around desperately, searching for anything that might help. *Shit*! If I hadn't taken the time to free the slaves, I'd still be able to run back and retrace my steps. I'd be able to find the matches wherever I dropped them.

Suddenly, I heard screams erupt from above me. Hundreds of screams, all shrill with panic. Hundreds became thousands. I smelled burning wood.

Blackstone had started the fire.

The screams got louder and louder as they spread through the entire crowd. The base of the Arena shook as thousands of spectators tried to evacuate.

And I still hadn't lit a single fuse.

Not knowing what else to do, I picked up a stone from the ground. I started striking my knife against it. Tiny sparks flew out. They did not have the energy to light the thick, heavy fuse.

I gritted my teeth and struck the rock harder. Again, and again, and again. I knew I was dulling my blade, but I had to get the fire lit. I concentrated all my energy on it…

Out of nowhere, a giant spark appeared. It hissed into the end of the fuse. The wick started to smoke.

I had no time to gloat in my success. I got up and ran, as fast as my leg could carry me, all the way to the next barrel.

I repeated what I had done the first time. Through fluke or sheer power of will, the third strike against the stone lit the fuse.

By now, the terrified screams above me were overbearing.

The fuses were long enough so that the last barrel would blow after twenty minutes. Each successive one was longer than the last, meaning they would all explode at the same time.

I lit the final one. Now, time was really working against me. I had to get up and find Blackstone.

I ran toward the exit—and stopped when I heard the frightened mewls of slaves coming from below me.

I looked down at the ducts. I'd freed the children in one room, but there were dozens more. I could not save them all.

The cries tore at me.

I looked up, heart racing. I knew this was a battle against the clock. Blackstone was waiting for me. He needed me beside him.

Suddenly, I had a moment of what I thought was absolute clarity. Blackstone was more experienced than I. He could take care of himself.

The slave children, on the other hand, could not.

That sealed my decision.

I changed paths and ran through the doors to burst into the second lower dungeon. The entire place shook from the ongoing stampede above us. Terrified wails added to the cacophony.

I skidded to a stop before the first cage. I jammed one of my knives into the lock and broke it open. The boy on the other side looked at me with empty eyes.

I flung the door open. "Come on!" I yelled, gesturing him outside.

He just sat there, at the far end of the cage, staring dumbly at me.

"Come on," I said again. "Get out!" I grabbed his arm to pull him.

He sunk sharp little teeth into my knuckles.

I yelped in surprise and ripped my hand back. The boy made no indication of moving. He simple stared at me with those dull, lifeless eyes.

A sense of urgency clawed at me. I knew that I should have been halfway up to Blackstone already.

But I couldn't just abandon the slaves. I'd been in their position. I knew what their lives were like. I could not let them die when the Arena blew.

I looked back at the cage. Surprise gripped me when I found the door closed again. The boy had reached out and pulled it shut!

I needed a collaborator. Someone who would help me. I looked around wildly, and found him.

He was small and ragged, like the rest. But he was the only one who gripped his cage bars and stared at me with intent eyes. I could tell he wanted to get out.

I ran over to him and broke the lock. I helped him out. I saw gratitude shine in his pupils.

"Here," I said. "Here, take this." I put my knife in his hand and brought him to the next cage over. I showed him how to guide the blade into the lock, twist, and pull it free.

Then I pushed him toward the others. "Go," I said. "Go!"

I didn't wait to see if he complied. I turned and sprinted out of the room.

A few levels higher I broke through a doorway right into a stampede of people. I looked up at the roof of the Arena, and saw flames licking the upper part of the structure. Black smoke fumed up and hid the highest suites from view.

I brought my shirt over my mouth and ran.

Screams sounded from all around me. I bumped and pushed through bodies as I went against the stream. Nobody paid me any mind. Nobody cared about a kid running toward his death.

The smoke thickened as I got higher. I hadn't reached the flames yet. Already I could feel their oppressive heat.

I saw stairs leading up. I took them two at a time, and emerged into a scene straight out of hell.

I was at the start of a long, wooden corridor. The entire thing was burning. Flames leapt from the sides and the floor. Smoke filled the air and made it impossible to breathe.

I dropped to my stomach and started to crawl. I tasted ash with every breath I took. The dirty air made me cough. Heat bombarded me from all sides. It was overwhelming. I did not know how I could get through with it beating so strongly against my body.

Then I remembered what Blackstone said. I could use the Flame of Souls to control my sleeping mind. I had used it only for pain before. But, if I could use it to lessen my perception of heat…

I knew it was risky. Subduing that sort of feeling meant I could hurt myself badly without knowing it. My clothes could catch fire, and I wouldn't notice the burning flesh on my back.

But, what choice did I have? Blackstone was relying on my help.

I stopped moving for a moment and concentrated. I piled all the sensations of heat into another small bundle in my mind. I pushed it together and ruthlessly stuffed it in the back, right next to the black ball of pain from my leg.

I will not lie. The feat did not come easy. Whereas with my leg, I could hold the pain back with little conscious effort, holding down *two* different sensations required more concentration than I could believe. The amount of mental power needed almost caused me to black out.

Somehow, I managed to open my eyes. And when I did, a kind of calm nirvana washed over me.

I saw the flames, yet felt no heat. I saw the smoke, yet could not smell it. My whole body felt numb, but it was still entirely under my control.

You know the feeling you get when you stand up too fast, and the blood pools away from your head? The one that takes a couple of seconds to recover from? When you're in that state, you do not feel fear. You do not feel anything, except for a vague kind of awareness of the lightness of your body.

That is something like what I experienced then—except I felt it an order of magnitude stronger. My body was my own. Yet, at the same time, it was not. There was no room for conscious thought left in my brain. Everything I did was purely on instinct.

I suspect that is how most horses live their lives.

I crawled forward. I would not say that time slowed for me, only that, all of a sudden, I was more aware of everything around me than I've ever been before. I could see the flames and predict where they would billow next. I could feel the flex of the floorboards and know which ones would give. It was like my brain was suddenly operating on another plane, much faster than it ever had before. Time did not slow, no.

I had merely transcended it.

I made it through the hallway unscathed. Pushing through the doors, I found a circular hall. The fire was not yet so bad on the other side.

Immediately, I knew why. Blackstone had rigged the hallway I'd just crawled through to burn first. He did it to prevent people from running up and interfering.

I scrambled to my feet, and let that second ball of sensation go. The heat roared into me. It wrapped around my body like a smothering cocoon. But I needed to have full access to my conscious mind.

Sounds of a fight erupted in my ears. They were coming from down the hall. I heard the shrill *ding* of metal upon metal.

A duel.

I ran.

I found a heavy door standing halfway open. Three bodies lay on the floor outside. Their throats were all cut.

I stepped over them and slipped inside.

I found Blackstone engaged in a bloody fight with none other than Three-Grin.

There were more bodies littered all over the floor. Two lay by the walls, while another four were crumpled over a large, locked chest in the back.

Neither man still alive noticed me. They were too busy with each other.

Three-Grin had a curved saber in either hand. The blades were stained red with blood. I looked at Blackstone, and was relieved to see that, aside from a scratch on his thigh, he was unharmed.

I saw the evil wounds cut into the bodies of the deceased, and everything made sense.

Blackstone and I were not the only ones with our eyes on the prize money. When the fire broke out, Three-Grin must have had the same thought. He'd butchered those protecting the chests in the mayhem. I do not know when Blackstone arrived. From the looks of the fight, it was not very long ago.

Blackstone had a two-handed sword in his hands. I had no idea where he'd gotten it. But, he was using it as well as one of his throwing blades. The sword met each one of Three-Grin's attacks strike for strike.

It was an even fight. The small cut on Blackstone's leg did not slow his movement. He thrust his sword up to defend Three-Grin's attacks, then launched a series of his own.

Three-Grin was a head taller than Blackstone. He'd ripped off his shirt sometime in the commotion, and I could see the thick, heavy muscle covering his body like armor. I would have thought the extra bulk would make him slow, but he danced on his feet just as easily as Blackstone.

The two men came at each other and separated. They came at each other and separated. The ring of steel against steel filled the room. Even though Three-Grin had two weapons, I saw him favoring the one in his right hand. He used it to launch his attacks. The one in his left only served to counter Blackstone's strikes.

Blades flashed through the air in a violent flurry. I had no idea that a man with a sword as big as Blackstone's could move so fast. He'd never taught me to use a proper sized weapon. All I had from him were my knives.

Three-Grin swung at Blackstone's head. The two-handed sword came up to parry the blow. Blackstone twisted his wrists, and the blade sliced downward, toward Three-Grin's shoulder.

The saber in Three-Grin's left hand came up to stop it inches away from his flesh. For a fraction of a second, Blackstone's large sword caught in the arc of Three-Grin's blade. As he moved to pull back, the second saber darted out and bit him in the side.

Blackstone grunted. That was the extent of his reaction. He twisted out of Three-Grin's reach. When his back turned to me I saw the damage Three-Grin had done.

There was a line of red running across Blackstone's oblique. It was not deep, but it was long. Already, the blood had started staining the cloth around it.

Three-Grin laughed and lunged again. Blackstone sidestepped the blow, driving his sword in a downward arc to send Three-Grin staggering. While he'd defended himself well, I saw him stumble a little as he turned around.

The second wound was slowing him.

Three-Grin spun back. Sensing his opponent weakened, he barreled toward him with full force. He used both his sabers to attack. They flickered, ducked, and twisted through the air, moving so fast that I could not even keep track.

Somehow, Blackstone repelled every single one.

From the length of my description you might get the impression that I'd been standing there, doing nothing, for a matter of minutes. That would be false. In truth, less than ten heartbeats had passed.

I knew I had to help. This was my chance to get my revenge against Three-Grin. This, *now*, was my opportunity. Here, in the Arena. Not in the tavern. Somehow, it felt more poetic to kill the man who defined my childhood in the place he'd sent me to die.

My legs moved without my brain telling them to. My knife slid into my hand. I ran straight into the heart of the battle.

There was no uncertainty holding me back. *This* is what I was

here to do. *This* is why I had raced to Blackstone. I ran, and when

I was within striking distance, I jumped.

My movement caught Blackstone's eye. "Dagan, no!" he

screamed. But, it was too late. I was already in the air.

I landed against Three-Grin's back. Triumph flared to life inside

me. I felt my blade sink into his thick skin. *This* is what I had

failed to do when I tried to save Alicia. *This* was the moment I'd

been dreaming of since.

My joy, however, was short-lived.

Three-Grin roared and spun around. The force of his spin threw

me off him. I crashed painfully into the chest. Pain exploded

beneath my armpit, and I thought I might have broken a rib. I

focused to stuff the sensation into the ball at the back of my

mind.

Then I watched, horrified, as Three-Grin reached back and pulled

out my knife without so much as a grimace.

He smiled viciously at me. "You think you can kill me?" he roared. He fended off Blackstone's next attack without looking his way. "You think you can kill one touched by Xune?"

His eyes shone with madness. Blackstone swung a side-sweep through the air, aimed toward Three-Grin's neck. The larger man lifted one forearm to block it. Blackstone's blade sank into Three-Grin's arm and stopped at the bone.

That seemed to drive Three-Grin further into the pits of insanity. Blackstone tried to jerk his sword out, but Three-Grin twisted his arm and wretched it from Blackstone's hands. Then, laughing, he swiped at Blackstone's exposed chest.

I cried out as the saber hit home. It cut a wide, deep gash from Blackstone's shoulder down to his navel.

Blackstone staggered, and fell.

Three-Grin threw his head back and laughed. It was a sound familiar to me from the dark dungeons. The crude noise filled my ears, mixing with the crackling flames all around me.

Three-Grin stepped toward me. My eyes darted around the room. The fire was starting to overtake the space. It had expanded from the outer hallway. Flames licked at the walls. Black smoke billowed to the ceiling. The heat in the room was immense.

I scrambled back, desperately trying to make sense of what I was seeing. *How* could Three-Grin have withstood my attack? I should have pierced his lung! Blackstone's sword still dangled from his arm, lodged right into the marrow of his bone. None of it slowed him.

Who was he?

My boot slipped as I tried to get up. I looked down, and saw blood leaking down my leg. I must have torn the stitches open.

Three-Grin reached me. He was a monstrous man. Right at that moment, he seemed larger than a mountain. The scars on his cheeks somehow came alive under those crazed eyes.

He pointed his saber at me. I looked at him and knew fear. I had failed.

He pushed the tip of his weapon into my shoulder. It was not enough to draw blood. But I felt the pressure nonetheless. He was toying with me.

Fire raged around us.

Three-Grin knelt down to my level. He looked at me through dark, glassy eyes.

They were the eyes of a madman.

"I remember you," he said. I wanted to squirm away, but he had me pinned like a bug. I breathed hard through gritted teeth. "You're the one adopted by my whore wife."

"By *Alicia*," I hissed, saying her name. "Who you killed!"

Three-Grin laughed. "She died because of you, boy. I should have known to kill you there. But Xune told me not to. He spoke to me, and said that you would make a great warrior in the Arena."

From the corner of my eye, I saw Blackstone staggering to his feet. He wavered as he stood.

"Your God is a lie," I spat at Three-Grin.

Three-Grin swung his head side to side madly. "Oh, really?" he said. "Tell me, then, why he grants *me* powers, and he brings to maggots like you… only *death*?"

Three-Grin pressed down on the blade. It slid into my shoulder.

I screamed. I did not scream because of the pain. I'd wrapped up the feeling to that part of my body the moment the saber touched me. I screamed because it was what Three-Grin wanted to hear. I screamed because I hoped it would give me time to think of *something* I could do.

Three-Grin rose, leaving the blade impaled in my shoulder. Behind him, Blackstone was getting closer. Blood soaked the front of his shirt. I was amazed he was still alive.

"Remember this?" Three-Grin laughed. He drew his leg back and kicked my side. I felt another rib crack. "Remember all the times I did this in the dungeons? Remember all the sacrifices I made to mighty Xune?"

His voice took on a crazed inflection as the kicks intensified. "Remember all the times you watched, hiding in that piss-stained corner of yours, as I killed the ones you knew? Remember my words, for they are the words of the Lord: *Xune sees all. Xune knows all. And Xune punishes all SINNERS!*"

He aimed a kick at my head. It caught me above the ear. My vision splintered and my hearing rang. I could see two of everything. Suddenly, the fire around us seemed so much worse.

Three-Grin stopped and grunted, seeming to notice the sword sticking out of his arm for the first time. He grabbed the blade, palm wrapped around the sharp edge, and pulled it out. It clattered to the floor.

Three-Grin showed me his hand. Blood poured down from a long cut across the middle. "Does this frighten you, boy?" he screamed. "Does my blood make you scared?" He laughed again, and then smeared the blood all over his face.

His laughter took on a maniacal quality.

He flipped his second saber over in his hand. His eyes bored into me. "And now," he said. "You die."

"No." Blackstone's voice. "You do, Three-Grin."

Blackstone swung the discarded long sword at Three-Grin's unprotected neck.

Everything seemed to happen at once.

Three-Grin twisted to block the attack. He moved faster than a striking cobra. Blackstone's sword rang off the curved metal edge of the saber inches from his neck. Three-Grin pivoted to his knees, jerked the second saber out of my shoulder, and thrust it deep into Blackstone's middle.

I screamed. "NO!"

At the same time, an enormous groan sounded from above us. I had only half a second to register it and leap back as a massive, burning wooden beam crashed from the ceiling onto the spot where I'd just been. The room shook on impact.

I staggered to my feet. I had to steady myself for a moment as my vision wobbled.

I saw two legs sticking out from under the beam. Three-Grin's legs.

They weren't moving.

I ran toward him, coughing in the smoke. The beam had fallen right on top of Three-Grin's body. It had broken his back!

I found Blackstone among the flames. He was kneeling down, clutching his stomach, but he was still alive.

The fire was starting to consume the entire room. Heat beat at me from every angle. Flames danced across the beam as I searched for a way to get across.

Blackstone's eyes shot up. He saw me. "Dagan," he choked. "Run."

Another beam groaned and crashed behind me.

"No!" I cried. "No! I won't leave you!" I staggered toward a gap in the flames, but they hissed and filled it just as I got there.

Heavy smoke thickened the room. I could barely breathe. I could not see Blackstone anymore. The fire raged unabated all around me.

"Dagan!" he called out from beyond the flames. "You have to run."

"No!"

"*RUN*!"

The command in his voice shook me. Another burning beam collapsed behind me. My head whipped back. I saw the last exit, still accessible. It wouldn't be for long. The doorway was burning. The pillars around it looked like they would give at any second.

A knife flew across my vision. It fell before it could reach the wall. Blackstone's amulet—the one he always wore around his neck—was fastened to the hilt.

"Run," his voice wavered.

I knelt down, clutched the amulet, and ran.

CHAPTER THIRTY-TWO

"I could not save him," Dagan muttered. "I could not get him out."

Earl took an uncomfortable swig of ale, and grimaced when he found the cup empty. He put it down as gently as he could, careful not to make a sound.

He had never seen Dagan so shaken. Clearly, reliving the tale had brought some very painful memories back to the surface.

"What about the gold?" Patch ventured.

Earl hissed at him and made a curt gesture with one hand. "Give him a moment's peace, boy!" he scolded.

The man in the hood shook his head. "No," he said. "No. Patch is right. That was long ago. I cannot mourn for the dead. Telling the story..." his hands gripped the table. Earl tried to ignore the thin tendrils of smoke that rose from beneath Dagan's fingertips.

"…brought me back. I was there again. I saw Three-Grin's mangled body under the post. I saw Blackstone on the other side. He was so close… the width of this table… but I could not… get to him."

Earl hesitated, then made up his mind and acted before he could change it. He reached across the table and put a hand on Dagan's shoulder.

"That was a hard loss," he said. "You couldn't have saved him."

Dagan tilted his head up. "You're wrong," he whispered. "I could have. If I hadn't stopped to free the slaves, Blackstone would still be alive. I'd have been there earlier. And Xune knows, the remainder of my life would have been very different."

"What happened to them?" Patch asked cautiously. "The slaves, I mean?"

Dagan barked a crude laugh. "What do you think? A few got out. Most were caught in the explosions. They didn't know which way to go. The ones that survived did not last long on the streets."

"Oh," Patch said, looking down.

"I told you before that this is not a tale of glory or redemption. It is the history of my life, as I have lived it. Trust me, Patch. Life is not a fairy tale."

Earl nodded his agreement. Dagan stirred, and Earl's courage failed him.

By gods, he thought, *I'm trying to comfort the Blind Assassin.*

With that, he withdrew his hand.

A strong wind howled outside. It was the kind of wind that gave children fright. But in those dark times, fear gripped grown men, too, for they knew the truth of the Things that came with the wind.

A gale blew the tavern door open. Everyone jumped at the crash.

Everyone, that is, except for the hooded man. He kept his eyes down, hidden in the shadows of his hood.

He knew that death would come tonight.

But it was not here yet.

THE END

Book One of

THE ASHES SAGA

About The Ashes Saga, Volume 2

Excited about the next book? Can't wait to read it?

That's great. Seriously, it means a lot to me.

I don't have a firm release day for it yet, but I'm aiming for late May or early June. Who knows, if writing goes really well, it might come out sooner.

But the best way to make sure you don't forget about it, with the least involvment from you, is to sign up for my new releases mailing list. I'll send out an email when the next book in The Ashes Saga comes out – nothing more.

Sign up here:

www.edwardmknight.com/mailing-list

Q&A with Edward M. Knight

Q: Who are you?

A: Just a guy who wrote a book.

Q: That's so vague.

A: But it's true.

Q: When's the next book coming out?

A: Soon. Late May or early June 2014. But if you were paying attention in the preceeding sections, you'd already know that ;)

Q: Is Blackstone really dead?

A: What do you think?

Q: I loved this freaking book. What do I do now?

A: Don't keep it to yourself. Tell your friends about it! The more people who know about it, the more motivated I am to write the sequels faster. It's win-win for everybody involved.

If you really want, you can email me your priase... but that effort is probably better spent telling people who *don't* know about the books about them.

(Yes, I know I'm using the plural form for just *one* book, but I intend to keep this series going for a while... assuming there's sufficient interest.)

My email: edward@edwardmknight.com

Q: I hated this book. What do I do?

A: Probably just forget about it. But if you're feeling particularly vindictive you can email me all the reasons why or leave many nasty reviews or do other things of that sort...

Q: Did you steal the idea for the Q&A from the back of Hugh Howey's *Wool* omnibus?

A: Why, yes. Yes, I did.

Q: Any other ways to get in touch?

A: Eventually I'll get around to setting up a FB page or a twitter profile or any of the dozens of horrific, social media time -sinks that exist in the world today. But honestly, how much of a media presence does an author need? All you guys care about should be my *books*.

Q: Anything parting words?

A: Yeah. I'm only 23, and plan on doing this writing gig for a long, long time. So if you liked what you read, you've got lots of books to look forward to in the future.

March 24, 2014.

ABOUT THE AUTHOR

Well, that's embarrasing. I don't actually have anything to put

here.

You'd be much better off just visiting my website and forming

your own opinion of me:

www.edwardmknight.com

Made in the USA
Charleston, SC
02 April 2014